A LECTURE ON THE
SANKHYA PHILOSOPHY

MAXWELL PRESS

A LECTURE ON THE
SANKHYA PHILOSOPHY

James Robert Ballantyne

MAXWELL PRESS

Chennai   New Delhi

MAXWELL PRESS

An Imprint of MJP Publishers

ISBN 978-93-5528-064-0   **MAXWELL PRESS**

All rights reserved
Printed and bound in India

No. 44, Nallathambi Street,
Triplicane,
Chennai 600 005

MJP 1366   © Publishers, 2022

Publisher :   **C. Janarthanan**

PUBLISHER'S NOTE

The legacy of a country is in its varied cultural heritage, historical literature, developments in the field of economy and science. The top nations in the world are competing in the field of science, economy and literature. This vast legacy has to be conserved and documented so that it can be bestowed to the future generation. The knowledge of this legacy is slowly getting perished in the present generation due to lack of documentation.

Keeping this in mind, the concern with retrospective acquiring of rare books has been accented recently by the burgeoning reprint industry. MAXWELL PRESS is gratified to retrieve the rare collections with a view to bring back those books that were landmarks in their time.

In this effort, a series of rare books would be republished under the banner, "MAXWELL PRESS". The books in the reprint series have been carefully selected for their contemporary usefulness as well as their historical importance within the intellectual. We reconstruct the book with slight enhancements made for better presentation, without affecting the contents of the original edition.

Most of the works selected for republishing covers a huge range of subjects, from history to anthropology. We believe this reprint edition will be a service to the numerous researchers and practitioners active in this fascinating field. We allow readers to experience the wonder of peering into a scholarly work of the highest order and seminal significance.

MAXWELL PRESS

PREFACE.

This Lecture, delivered in the session of 1849, is a sequel to those on the *Nyáya* Philosophy delivered to the senior class of pupils in the English Department of the Benares College, in 1848, "with the view of introducing them to the philosophical terminology current among their learned fellow-countrymen the pandits."

For selecting the *Tattwa-samása* as the text-book, there were two motives—the simplicity of its arrangement, and the extreme rarity of the work. Mr. Colebrooke (at p. 233. vol. 1st of his Essays) speaks of it as being uncertain whether the work were still extant; and few of the pandits appear to know it except by name.

J. R. B.

Benares College,
31*st July,* 1850.

PREFACE.

Tʜɪꜱ Lecture, delivered in the session of 1849, is a sequel to those on the *Nyáya* Philosophy delivered to the senior class of pupils in the English Department of the Benares College, in 1848, " with the view of introducing them to the philosophical terminology current among their learned fellow-countrymen the pandits."

For selecting the *Tattwa-samása* as the text-book, there were two motives—the simplicity of its arrangement, and the extreme rarity of the work. Mr. Colebrooke (at p. 233. vol. 1st of his Essays) speaks of it as being uncertain whether the work were still extant; and few of the pandits appear to know it except by name.

J. R. B.

Benares College,
31*st July*, 1850.

SYNOPSIS OF THE CONTENTS.

The twenty-five Principles—consisting of—

No. 5.—THE EIGHT PRODUCERS :—

      Viz. No. 6.—The Undiscrete—

      ,, No. 8.—Intellect—

      ,, No. 17.—Self-consciousness—

      ,, No. 19.—The five Subtile Elements—

No. 26.—THE SIXTEEN PRODUCTIONS :—

      Viz. No. 27.—The eleven Organs—

      ,, No. 31.—The five Gross Elements—

No. 34.—SOUL.

The operation of the Principles—consisting in

No. 54.—Developement—

No. 55.—Reabsorption—

No. 73.—Bondage—

No. 74.—Liberation.

The Sánkhya theory of Evidence—involving

No. 76.—Perception—

No. 77.—Inference—

No. 78.—Testimony.

A LECTURE

ON THE

SANKHYA PHILOSOPHY.

No. 1.—[THE founder of the *Sánkhya* school of philosophy was
Kapila. Two treatises are attributed to him—the *Sánkhya-pra-
vachana* and the *Tatwa-samása*. The latter will form the text
of the following observations. The commentary commences
thus :—]

श्री गणेशाय नमः । श्री कपिलमुनये नमः । पञ्चविंशति त-
त्त्वेषु जन्मना ज्ञानमाप्तवान् । आदिसृष्टौ नमस्तस्मै कपिलाय
महर्षये ॥

अथातत्त्वसमासाख्यसांख्यसूत्राणि व्याख्यास्यामः ॥

No. 2.—Salutation to *Ganes'a !* Salutation to the great sage
Kapila ! Salutation to that great sage *Kapila* who, at the first
creation, obtained, merely by birth, a knowledge of the twenty-
five principles (*tatwa*).

Now we shall explain the aphorisms of the *Sánkhya,* which constitute what is called the Compendium of Principles.

[In saying that *Kapila* obtained his knowledge "merely by
birth," the author means that *Kapila* differed from those other tea-

A

chers who, after being born, received instruction before they were qualified to teach. *Kapila* is regarded as an incarnation of the deity.]

इह कश्चिद्‌ब्राह्मणस्त्रिविधेन दुःखेनाभिभूतः सांख्याचार्यं कपि-
लमहर्षिं शरणमुपागतः । स्वकुलनामगोत्रं स्वाध्यायार्थं निवे-
द्याच । भगवन् किमिह परं। किं याथातथ्यं । किं कृत्वा कृतकृत्यः
स्यामिति । कपिल उवाच । कथयिष्यामि ।

No. 3.—A certain bráhman, aggrieved by the three kinds of pain, had recourse to the great sage *Kapila*, the teacher of the *Sánkhya*. Having declared his family, his name and race, and his desire of instruction, he said—" Holy Sir ! What is of all things the most important ? What is actual truth ? And what must I do in order that I may have done what is fitting to be done ?" *Kapila* replied—" I shall tell you."

[The Aphorisms of *Kapila* here follow.]

अष्टौ प्रकृतयः ।१॥ षोडश विकाराः ।२॥ पुरुषः ।३॥ त्रैगु-
ण्यं ।४॥ संचरः ।५॥ प्रतिसंचरः ।६॥ अध्यात्मं ।७॥ अधिभूतं
।८॥ अधिदैवतं ।९॥ पञ्चाभिबुद्धयः ।१०॥ पञ्च कर्मयोनयः ।
११॥ पञ्च वायवः ।१२॥ पञ्च कर्मात्मानः ।१३ ॥ पञ्चपर्वावि-
द्या ।१४॥ अष्टाविंशतिधाशक्तिः ।१५॥ नवधा तुष्टिः ।१६॥ अष्ट-
धा सिद्धिः ।१७॥ दशधा मूलिकार्थाः ।१८॥ अनुग्रहसर्गः ।१९॥
चतुर्दशविधो भूतसर्गः ।२०॥ त्रिविधो धातुसंसर्गः ।२१॥ त्रिवि-
धो बन्धः ।२२॥ त्रिविधो मोक्षः ।२३॥ त्रिविधं प्रमाणं ।२४॥

चिविधं दु:खं ।२५॥ एतद्याथातथ्यं । एतत्सम्यक् ज्ञात्वा कृतकृ-
त्य: स्यात् न पुनस्त्रिविधेन दु:खेनाभिभूत इति तत्त्वसमासाख्य-
सांख्यसूचानि ॥

No. 4.—"(1) The eight 'producers' (prakriti) ; (2) the six-
"teen 'productions' (vikára) ; (3) 'Soul' (purusha); (4) the
"'triad of qualities' (traigunya); (5) 'emanation' or 'develope-
"ment' (sanchara); (6) 're-absorption' or 'dissolution' (prátisan-
"chara); (7) the 'ministers of Soul' (adhyátma) ; (8) the 'pro-
"vince of an organ' (adhibhúta); (9) the respective 'presiding
"deity' (adhidaivata) ; (10) the five 'perversities of understand-
"ing" (abhibuddhi) ; (11) the five 'sources of action' (karmma-
"yoni); (12) the five 'airs' (váyu) ; (13) the five 'which consist
"of action' (karmmátma) ; (14) 'ignorance' (avidyá) under five
"divisions ; (15) 'disability' (as'akti) of twenty-eight kinds ; (16)
"'acquiescence' or 'indifference' (tushṭi) of nine kinds ; (17)
"'perfectness' (siddhi) of eight kinds ; (18) the 'radical facts'
"(mulikártha) of ten kinds ; (19) 'benevolent nature,' (anugra-
"ha-sarga) ; (20) 'created existences' (bhúta-sarga) of ten des-
"criptions ; (21) 'parental creation' (dhátu-sansarga) of three dis-
"criptions ; (22) three-fold 'bondage' (bandha) ; (23) three-fold
"'liberation' (moksha) ; (24) three-fold 'proof' (pramána) ; (25)
"three-fold 'pain' (du'kha):— in this consists all actual truth.
"He who shall have thoroughly understood this, will have done
"all that is to be done. He will not again be obnoxious to the
"three sorts of pain."

Such are the Aphorisms of the Sánkhya, entitled the 'Compendium of Principles.'

[The commentator then proceeds to dilate on each of the foregoing topics.]

तच्चाव्यक्तं तावदुच्यते । यथा लोके व्यज्यन्ते घटपटकुटशयनका-
द्या न तथा व्यज्यते इत्यव्यक्तं । श्रोत्रादिभिरिन्द्रियैर्न गृह्यते
इत्यर्थः । कस्मात् । अनादिमध्यान्तत्वान्निरवयवत्वाच्च । अभ-
व्दमसर्वंमरूपमव्ययन्तथाच नित्यं रसगन्धवर्ज्जितं । अनादिमध्य-
मह्तः परं ध्रुवं प्रधानमेतत्प्रवदन्ति सूरयः । सूक्ष्ममलिंगमनादि-
निधनं तथाप्रसवधर्मि निरवयवमेकमेव हि साधारणमेतदव्यक्तं ।

No. 6.—Now the 'undiscrete' is described. As, in this
world, jars, webs, vases, and couches are made manifest, not so
is the 'undiscrete':—that is to say—it is not apprehended by the
hearing or by any other sense. Why? Because it has neither beginning, middle, nor end; nor is it made up of parts. The inaudible,
intangible, invisible, indestructible, and likewise eternal, devoid
of savour and odour,—without beginning or middle, anterior in order to mind, firm and chief—thus do the learned designate it.
Subtile, devoid of characteristic attributes, unconscious, without
beginning or end,—so too whose nature it is to produce, without
parts, one only, the common [source of all]—such is the 'undiscrete.'

अव्यक्तस्यामी पर्य्यायशब्दा भवन्ति । अव्यक्तं । प्रधानं । ब्रह्म ।
पुरं । ध्रुवं । प्रधानकं । अच्चरं । च्चेच्चं । तमः । प्रसतमिति ।

No. 7.—Synonymes of the 'undiscrete' are the following—viz :
the 'undistinguished,' 'unseparated,' or 'imperceptible' (*avyak-
ta*); the 'chief' (*pradhána*); the 'source of emanation' (*brahma*):
the 'receptacle' or 'abode,' (*pura*); the 'permanent' (*dhruva*) ;
the 'chief,' or 'that in which all generated effect is comprehen-
ded' (*pradhánaka*); the 'indestructible' (*akshara*) ; the 'site' or
'field' (*kshetra*); 'darkness' (*tamas*); the 'productive source' (*pra-
súta*).

[Several of these terms are not, strictly speaking, synonymes,
further than as they are all applicable to the 'undiscrete'. They
are epithets employed for reasons which may appear in the sequel.
A similar remark applies to the various lists of synonymes which
will be met with further on.

We now come to the second of the eight 'producers' (No. 5)
—viz 'intellect'.]

का बुद्धिरुच्यते । अध्यवसायो बुद्धिः । सा ऽयमध्यवसा-
यो गवादिषु द्रव्येषु यस्मात्प्रतिपत्तिः । एवमेतन्नान्यथा । गौरे-
वायं नाश्वः । स्थाणुरेवायं न पुरुषः । इत्येषा बुद्धिः ।

No. 8.—What is 'intellect'? To this it is replied—'intellect'
is 'ascertainment' *(adhyavasáya)*. This it is from which, in regard to a cow or any other thing, there is the determination
'This is so and so, and not otherwise'—'This is a cow, not a
horse'—'This is a post, not a man.' Such is 'intellect' or 'understanding.'

[The various aspects under which this faculty is regarded as
presenting itself, are next specified.]

तच धर्मौ नामाधर्मविपर्यय: श्रुतिस्मृतिविहित: शिष्टाचारा-
विरुद्ध: शुभलच्चण: ।

No. 10.—' Virtue' (*dharma*) is the opposite of 'vice'. (*adharma*) ;
it is what is enjoined in the ' scripture' (*s'ruti*) and in the ' law'
(*smriti*) ; not opposed to the practice of the pious—of which the
symptom is felicity [—prosperity being regarded as the fruit of
former virtue, and adversity as that of former vice.]

च्ञानं नामाच्ञानविपर्यय: । तत्वभावभूतानां सम्बोध: ।

No. 11,—' Knowledge' (*jnyána*) is the opposite of ' ignorance'
(*ajnyána*)—an acqaintance with the ' principles' (*tatwa*), the
' forms' of intellect (*bháva*-No. 9.), and the 'elements' (*bhúta*-
No 31.)

वैराग्यं नामावैराग्यविपर्यय: । शब्दादिविषयेष्वप्रसक्ति: ।

No. 12.—' Dispassion' (*vairágya*) is the opposite of ' passion'
(*avairágya*) :—it consists in not concerning one's self about
sounds or any other ' objects of sense' (*vishaya*).

ऐश्वर्यं नामानैश्वर्यंविपर्यय: । अणिमादयो ऽष्टगुणा: । ए-
तानि साल्विकानि चत्वारि ।

No. 13.—Superhuman ' power' (*aiswurya*) is the opposite of
' powerlessness' (*anaiswarya*) ; it consists of the eight qualities,

[the capacity of assuming a form of the utmost] 'minuteness' (*aṇimá*) &c.

These four [kinds of 'intellect'—Nos. 10.—13.] are [regarded as] 'partaking of the quality of goodness' (*sátwika*). [See No. 50].

अधर्मो ऽज्ञानमवैराग्यमनैश्वर्यमिति । अधर्मो नाम धर्मविपर्य-
यः । श्रुतिस्मृतिविरुद्धः । शिष्टाचारविरुद्धः । अशुभलक्षणः । अ-
ज्ञानं नाम ज्ञानविपर्ययः । तत्त्वभावभूतानामनवबोधः । अवैरा-
ग्यं नाम वैराग्यविपर्ययः । शब्दादिविषयेष्वभिनिवेशः । अनैश्व-
र्यं नाम ऐश्वर्यविपर्ययः । अणिमादिरहितत्वं । एतानि तामसा-
नि चत्वारि ।

No. 14.—'Vice' (*adharma*), 'ignorance' (*ajnyána*), 'subjeetion to passion' (*avairágya*), and 'powerlessness' (*anaiswarya*), [are next described].

'Vice' is the opposite of 'virtue'—opposed to Scripture and Law—opposed to the practice of the pious—and of which the symptom is adversity. [See No. 10].

'Ignorance' is the opposite of 'knowledge'—the reverse of an acquaintance with the 'principles', the 'forms' of intellect, and the 'elements'. [See No. 11.]

'Subjection to passion' is the opposite of 'dispassion' :—it consists in perseveringly concerning one's self about sounds and other objects of sense.

'Powerlessness' is the opposite of superhuman 'power':—it is the being destitute of [the capacity of] 'minuteness' &c.

These four [kinds of 'intellect'] are [regarded as] 'partaking of the quality of Darkness' (*támasa*). [See No. 52].

[What consequences severally appertain to the above-described modifications of 'intellect,' is next stated.]

तच्च धर्मेण निमित्तेनोर्ध्वंगमनं । ज्ञानेन निमित्तेन मोच्छः । वैराग्येण निमित्तेन प्रकृतिलयः । ऐश्वर्वनिमित्तेनाप्रतिहतगति-र्भवति । एवमेषा अष्टरूपा बुद्धिः परिख्याता ।

No. 15.—Through 'virtue,' as a cause, there is 'elevation in the scale of being' (*úrdhwa-gamana*); through 'knowledge,' as a cause, there is 'liberation' from existence (*moksha*); through 'dispassion,' as a cause, there is 'absorption into nature,' (*prakriti-laya*); through superhuman 'power,' as a cause, there is 'unimpeded movement' [even through solid rocks and the like], (*iapratihata-gati*).

Thus has 'intellect,' in its eight forms [No. 9] been described.

बुद्धेरमी पर्यायशब्दा भवन्ति ।

मनो मतिर्महान् ब्रह्मा ख्यातिः प्रज्ञा श्रुतिर्धृतिः । प्रज्ञानस-न्ततिः स्मृतिर्धीर्बुद्धिः परिकथ्यते ॥

No. 16.—The following words are synonymes—[See No. 7]—of 'intellect'—viz : 'mind' (*manas*); 'understanding' (*mati*); the 'great' principle (*mahat*); the 'Creator' (*brahmá*) ; 'familiar knowledge' (*khyáti*); 'wisdom' (*prajnyá*); 'intelligence through report' (*s'ruti*); 'resolution' (*dhriti*); a 'train of thought' (*prajnyáná-santati*); 'memory' (*smriti*); and 'meditation' (*dhí*); in such terms is 'intellect' spoken of.

[We now come to the third of the eight 'producers' (No. 5)—viz 'self-consciousness'—that which is implied in a man's employing the pronoun 'I'—a pronoun the employment of which declares the speaker's belief that he possesses an individuality of his own.]

अथ को ऽहंकार इत्युच्यते । अभिमानो ऽहंकारः ।
यो ऽयमभिमानः । अहं शब्दे अहं स्पर्शे अहं रूपे अहं रसे ।
अहं गन्धे अहं स्वामी धनवानहमीश्वरः । अहं भोगी अहं धर्मे ऽभि-
यक्तो ऽसौ मया हतः । अहं हनिष्ये बलिभिः परैरित्येवमादिकः
प्रत्ययो यः सो ऽहंकारः ।

No. 17.—To the question—what is 'self-consciousness'?—it is replied that 'self-consciousness' is a 'conceit' (*abhimána*)—the conceit or fancy that 'I am the embracer in the case of sound' [i. e., 'I hear'], 'I feel,' 'I see,' 'I taste,' 'I am lord,' 'I am rich,' 'I am deity,' 'I enjoy,' 'I am connected with virtue,' 'by *me* was he slain,' 'I shall be slain by powerful enemies :'—such and the like belief is 'self-consciousness.'

[The term *ahankára* (the 'making of an *Ego* or an *I')*, the technical import of which, as remarked by Professor Wilson, is 'the pride or conceit of individuality,'* is rendered, in Mr. Colebrooke's version of the *Sánkhya Káriká*, by the term 'Egotism.' It must be carefully borne in mind that the word 'egotism,' thus employed, is not to carry with it the familiar import of bustling vanity—the feeling which prompts a vain man to be constantly talking about himself :—for, a man who is no 'egotist,' in that familiar sense of the term, is not the less chargeable with *ahan-kára*, if he fancies that his employing the pronoun 'I' at all is not an absurdity. The word, as described by *Váchaspati*, in his commentary on the 24th of the *Káríkás* of *I's'wara Krishna*, might signify 'egotism' in the ordinary sense—verging even on 'ego-ism,' —i.e., the belief that ' besides me there is nought else :'—but the significance of *Kapila's* system will perhaps be more clearly dis-

---

dent of inference' (*niranumána*).

[Of the eight ' producers' (No. 5) we have now to consider the last five—viz., the five ' subtile elements'—the rudiments of what are familiarly called the ' elements.']

अथाह कानि पञ्च तन्माचाणीत्युच्यते । अहंकारान्वितानि प-
ञ्च तन्माचाणि । शब्दतन्माचं स्पर्शतन्माचं रूपतन्माचं रसत-
न्माचं गन्धतन्माचञ्चेति पञ्च तन्माचाणि ।

No. 19.—To the question—what are the five ' subtile elements' ?—it is replied :—the five ' subtile elements' are consequents of ' self-consciousness.' The ' subtile element of sound' (*s'abda-tanmátra*) ; the ' subtile element of tangibility' (*spars'a-tanmátra*) ; the ' subtile element of colour' (*rúpa-tanmátra*) ; the ' subtile element of savour' (*rasa-tanmátra*) ; and the ' subtile element of odour' (*gandha-tanmátra*) ;—these are the five ' subtile elements.'

[" *Tan-mátra* is a compound of *tad*, ' that,' and *mátra*, ' alone ;' implying, that in which its own peculiar property resides, without any change or variety." In this respect the ' subtile elements' are held to differ from the gross or derivative elements, the properties of which are various at different times and in respect to different mortals.]

तच तावच्छब्दतन्माचाणि शब्देष्वेवोपलभ्यन्ते । उदात्तानुदा-
त्तस्वरितकस्मिनघड़ुर्षभगान्धारमध्यमपञ्चमधैवतनिषादादय: श-
ब्दविशेषा उपलभ्यन्ते । तस्माच्छब्दतन्माचे ऽ विशेष: ।

No. 20.—The 'subtile elements of sound' [like the 'atoms' of the Nyáya, which are separately inappreciable by the senses of men,] are apprehended only in [derivative and gross] ' sounds.' Varieties of ' sound' are apprehended, such as ' acutely accented,' ' gravely accented,' 'circumflexly accented,' and [the notes of the gamut—viz. :] 'C' (*shadja*), 'D' (*rishabha*), ' E' (*gándhára*), 'F' (*madhyama*—i. e., the ' middle' note of the scale—correspond-ing to the ' sub-dominant'*), ' G' (*panchama*—i.e. the 'fifth' note of the scale—corresponding to the ' dominant'), ' A' (*dhaivata*), 'B' (*nisháda*), &c. But there is not hence [i. e., in accordance with the variety in sounds appreciable by mortals] any diversity in the ' subtile element of sound' itself.

---

* It is noticeable that the keynote and those two important notes, the do-minant and sub-dominant, have names marking their place in the scale, whilst the other names are unscientific and fantastical. The word *rishabha* means ' a bull,' *gándhára* means 'red lead,' *dhaivata* seems to have no sense elsewhere, and *nisháda* means 'an outcaste.' The keynote—viz., *shad-ja* 'born of six' is said to be so named because it is "supposed to require for its articu-lation the employment of the tongue, teeth, palate, nose, throat and teeth,"— but this is evidently the conjecture of a grammarian, not of a musician. The writers on music may have given it the name as indicative of the acoustic fact that the ear, though content if the keynote be sounded, demands that, if the other six are sounded in their order, the keynote shall follow (before clo-sing) to complete the octave and to form the cadence. It is " the offspring of (all or any of these) six."

In these, varieties of ' tangibility' are apprehended—such as ' soft,' ' hard,' ' rough,' ' slippery,' ' cold,' ' hot,' &c. But there is not hence any diversity in the ' subtile element of tangibility' itself.

रूपतन्माचाणि रूपेष्वेवोपलभ्यन्ते । तच मुक्तरक्तकृष्णहरित-
पीतहारिद्रमांजिष्ठाद्यो रूपविश्रेषा उपलभ्यन्ते । तस्माद्रूपतन्मा-
चेऽविश्रेषः ।

No. 22.—The ' subtile elements of colour' are apprehended only in ' colours.' In these, varieties of ' colour' are apprehended—such as ' white,' ' red,' ' black,' ' green,' ' yellow,' ' turmeric-colour,' ' madder-colour,' &c. But there is not hence any diversity in the ' subtile element of colour' itself.

रसतन्माचाणि रसेष्वेवोपलभ्यन्ते । तच कटुतिक्तकषायच्वा-
रमधुराम्ललवणाद्यो रसविश्रेषा उपलभ्यन्ते । तस्माद्रसतन्माचे
ऽविश्रेषः ।

No. 23.—The ' subtile elements of savour' are apprehended only in ' savours.' In this, varieties of ' savour' are apprehended—such as 'pungent,' 'bitter,' 'astringent,' 'alkaline,' 'sweet,' ' acid,' ' salt,' &c. But there is not hence any diversity in the ' subtile element of savour' itself.

गन्धतन्माचाणि गन्धे एवोपलभ्यन्ते । तच्च सुरभिरसुरभिस्च
गन्धविग्रेषौ उपलभ्येते । तस्माङ्गन्धतन्माचे ऽ विग्रेष: । एव-
मेतत्पञ्चतन्माचाणि सूचितानि ।

No. 24.—The ‘ subtile elements of odour’ are apprehended
only in ‘ odour.’ In this, two varieties of ‘ odour’—viz., ‘ fra-
grance’ and ‘ stench,’ are apprehended. But there is not hence
any diversity in the ‘ subtile element of odour’ itself.

Thus have the five ‘ subtile elements’ been made known.

अथैषां पर्यायशब्दा: । तन्माचाणि अविग्रेषाणि मद्याभतानि
प्रक्कतयो ऽभोग्यानि अणवोऽग्रान्ताघोरामूढानीति । एवमेता अ-
व्यक्तबुद्ध्यहंकारतन्माचसंज्ञिता अष्टौ प्रक्तयो व्याख्याता: । अ-
ग्र कस्मात्प्रक्तय: । प्रकुर्वन्तीति प्रक्तय: ।

No. 25.—Now the synonymes of these are ‘elemental rudiments’ (tan-mátra); ‘ unvaried’ (avis'esha); the ‘ pervading elements’ or ‘whence the gross elements proceed’ (mahá-bhúta) ;
‘producers’ (prakriti) ; ‘not adapted for [mortal] fruition’ (a-
bhogya) ; ‘ atoms’ (anu) ; ‘not soothing’ (as'ánta) ; ‘not terrific’
(aghora) ; ‘ not stupifying’ (amúdha). [These last three names
refer to the triad of Qualities—see No. 49]. Thus have the
eight producers—viz., the ‘undiscrete,’ ‘intellect,’ ‘ self-cousious-
ness,’ and the five ‘subtile elements,’ been explained.

Now why are these (No. 5) called ‘producers’ ? It is because
they produce [the sixteen ‘ productions’—see No. 4—which are
next to be described.]

अथ ते के षोडश विकारा इत्यत्रोच्यते । एकादशेन्द्रियाणि पञ्च
भूतान्येते षोडश विकारा: ।

it is replied :—the eleven 'organs' (*indriya*), and the five [derivative or gross] 'elements:'—these are the sixteen 'productions,' or 'modifications' [*vikára*].

तचेन्द्रियाणि तावदुच्यन्ते । श्रोचं त्वक्चचुषी जिह्वा घ्राणमि-
ति पञ्च बुद्वीन्द्रियाणि ।

No. 27.—Now the 'organs' are set forth. The 'organ of hearing' (*s'rotra*); the 'organ of touch' (*twach*) and the 'organ of sight' (*chakshush*); the 'organ of taste' (*jihwá*); the 'organ of smell' (*ghrána*); are the five 'organs of the intellect' (*buddhíndriya*).

(These are called 'organs of the intellect' because their function is that of observation, not, as that of the other organs is, of action.)

श्रोचं शब्दविषयं बुध्यते । त्वक् स्पर्शविषयं बुध्यते । चचूरूप-
विषयं बुध्यते । रसना रसविषयं बुध्यते । घ्राणो गन्धविषयं
बुध्यते । इति

No. 28.—The 'hearing' apprehends its object 'sound' (*s'abda*). The 'touch' apprehends its object 'tangibility' (*spars'a*). The 'sight' apprehends its object 'colour' (*rúpa*). The 'taste' apprehends its object 'savour' (*rasa*). The 'smell' apprehends its object 'odour' (*gandha*).

वाक् पाणिपादम् पायूपस्थाख्यानि पञ्च कर्मेन्द्रियाणि सं खंक-
र्म्म कुर्वन्ति । वाक् वचनमुच्चरति । हस्तौ कर्म कुरुतः । पादौ
विहरणम् । पायुर्विसर्गम् । उपस्थम् आनन्दम् । उभयात्मकं मनः
स्वसंकल्पविकल्पवृत्ती कुरुते । एवमेकादशेन्द्रियाणि व्याख्यातानि ।

No. 29.—The five ' organs of action' (*karmendriya*), viz., the
' voice' or the ' larynx &c.' (*vák*), the ' hands,' the ' feet,' the
' organ of excretion,' and the ' organ of generation,' perform
severally their own function. The ' voice' pronounces words.
The ' hands' perform actions. The ' feet' perform locomotion ;
the ' organ of excretion,' evacuation ; and the ' organ of generation,' enjoyment. ' Mind' (*manas*), an organ both of observation and action, performs its appropriate functions of ' resolving'
(*sankalpa*) and ' doubting' (*vikalpa*).

Thus have the eleven organs been described.

ऋथैवं पर्य्यायाः । इन्द्रियाणि करणानि वैकारिकाणि नियतानि
पदानि अवधृतानि अणूनि अच्चाणीति ।

No. 30.—Now the synonymes of these are—'organs of sense'
(*indriya*); ' instruments' (*karana*) ; ' changers' (*vaikárika*) ; ' al-
lotted' (to each mortal) (*niyata*) ; ' appliances' (*pada*) ; 'placed
under' (the soul) (*avadhrita*) ; ' subtile' (*anu*) ; 'organs' (*aksha*).

ऋथ कानि पञ्च मद्दाभूतानीत्यचोच्यते । एथिव्यप्तेजोवाय्वाका-
शानीति मद्दाभूतानि ।

No. 31.—Now what are the five ' gross elements' (*mahá-bhúta*)? To this it is replied—' earth,' ' water,' 'light,' ' air,' and
ether,' are the 'gross elements.'

तच्च एथिवी धारणभावेन प्रवर्त्तमाना चतुर्णामुपकारं करोति ।
आपः जलानि क्लेदनभावेन प्रवर्त्तमानानि चतुर्णामुपकारं कुर्वन्ति ।
तेजः पाचकभावेन प्रवर्त्तमानं चतुर्णामुपकारं करोति । वायुः
शोषणभावेन प्रवर्त्तमानस्तुर्णां मुपकारं करोति । आकाश अ-

वकाशदानेन प्रवर्त्तमानं चतुर्णामुपकारं करोति । शब्दस्पर्शरूप-
रसगन्धवती पञ्चगुणा पृथिवी । शब्दस्पर्शरूपरसवत्यश्चतुर्गुणा आ-
पः । शब्दस्पर्शरूपवत्त्रिगुणं तेजः । शब्दस्पर्शवानिति द्विगुणो वा-
युः । शब्दवदेकगुणमाकाशम् । एवमाख्यातानि पञ्च महाभूतानि ।

No. 32.—'Earth,' acting in the character of supporter, co-operates with the [other] four [elements, in the production of effects.' 'Water' acting in its character of the 'humid,' co-operates
with the other four. 'Light,' acting in the way of 'maturation,'
co-operates with the other four. 'Air,' acting in the way of
'siccation,' co-operates with the other four. 'Ether,' acting
in the way of giving space, co-operates with the other four.

'Earth' is possessed of five qualities—having 'sound,' 'tangibility,' 'colour,' 'savour,' and 'odour.' 'Water,' possesses 'sound,' 'tangibility,' 'colour,' and 'savour.' 'Light' possesses 'sound,' 'tangibility,' and 'colour.' 'Air' possesses 'sound' and 'tangibility.'
'Ether' has the single quality of 'sound.'

Thus have the 'gross' 'elements' been set forth.

अथैषां पर्यायाः । भूतानि । भूतविशेषाः । विकाराः । आकृ-
तयः । तनवः । विग्रहाः । शान्ताः । घोराः । मूढाः । इत्येते
षोडश विकारा व्याख्याताः ।

No. 33.—Now their synonymes—'elements' (*bhúta*), 'varieties
of element' (*bhúta-vis'esha*), ' productions' or ' modifications'
(*vikára*), 'forms' (*ákriti*), 'minute,' (*tanu*), bodies, (*vigraha*), ' soo-
' thing,' ' terrific,' ' stupifying.'

[The eight 'producers,' and the sixteen 'productions,' or results of the modification of the ' producers,' having been thus described, the third of *Kapila's* aphorisms, in which he announces ' soul,' is next adverted to.]

अथाह कः पुरुषः । इत्युच्यते । पुरुषो ऽनादिः सूक्ष्मः सर्वगतस्वे-तनो ऽगुणो नित्यो द्रष्टा भोक्ता ऽकर्त्ता चेचबिदमलो ऽप्रसवध-र्मीति ।

No. 34.—Now it is asked—what is ' soul' ? To this it is replied —' soul' is without beginning, subtile, omnipresent, intelligent, without [the three] qualities [see No. 49], eternal, spectator, enjoyer, not an agent, the knower of body, pure, not producing aught.

अथाह कस्मात्पुरुषः । पुराणात् पुरि शयनात् पुरोहितवृत्ति-त्वाच्च पुरुषः ।

No. 35.—Now it is asked—why [is it called] ' soul' (*purusha*)? Because it is ' ancient' (*purána*) [having been from eternity—see No. 34—]; and because ' it reposes in body' (*puri s'ayate*); and because it is that towards which the ' highest affection' (*puro hita*) is entertained [—seeing that each one loves *self*, if loving nought else—] therefore it is called *purusha*.

अथ कस्मादनादिः । नास्यादिरन्तो मध्यो वा विद्यते इत्यना-दिः । कस्मात्सूक्ष्मः । निरवयवत्वादतीन्द्रियत्वात्सूक्ष्मः । कस्मा-त्सर्वगतः । सर्वमाप्नवाननन्तास्देा गगनवदस्तोति सर्वगतः । क-स्माचेतनः । सुखदुःखमोहेापलब्धिमत्त्वात् । कस्मादगुणः । सत्वर-जक्तमांस्यस्मिन् सन्त्यतो ऽगुणः । कस्मान्नित्यः । अकृतकत्वादनु-

Why 'subtile'? From its being without parts, and its transcending the senses. Why 'omnipresent'? Because it comes into relation with all, and its sphere is boundless as the sky. Why 'intelligent'? From its discerning pleasure, pain, and delusion. Why 'without qualities'? Because neither the quality of 'goodness' [No. 49], of 'passion,' nor of 'darkness,' is in it. Why 'eternal'? From its not being made or produced. Why 'spectator'? Because it apprehends the modifications which productive nature undergoes. Why 'enjoyer'? Because it discerns pleasure and pain through its possession of intelligence. Why 'not an agent'? From its being indifferent (*udásína*) and devoid of the 'qualities' [see No. 42.] Why the 'knower of body'? Because through bodies it apprehends the 'qualities.' Why 'pure'? Because in this 'soul' there are neither good actions nor bad. Why 'not wont to produce'? Because it is seedless :—that is to say, it does not give rise to any thing.

Thus has the 'soul' of the *Sánkhya* been described?

अथास्य पुरुषस्य पर्यायाः । पुरुषः । आत्मा । पुमान् । पंगुण-जन्तजीवः । चेतनः । नरः । कविः । ब्रह्म । अक्षरः । प्राणः ।

य: । क: । स: । एष: । एवमेतानि पञ्चविंशति तत्वानि व्या-
ख्यातानि । अष्टौ प्रकृतयः षोडश विकाराः पुरुषश्चेति ।

पञ्चविंशतितत्वज्ञो यत्रकुत्राश्रमे रतः ।

जटी शिखी मुण्डी वापि मुच्यते नाच संशयः ॥

No. 37.—Now the synonymes of this 'soul'—the 'reposer in
body' *(purusha)*; 'self' *(átmá)*; 'the male' *(puns)*; 'that which
superadds the quality of reason to mere animal life' *(pun-guna-
jantu-jíva)*; the 'knower of body' *(kshetra-jna)*; the 'man' *(na-
ra)*; the 'poet' *(kavi)*; 'deity' *(brahma)*; the 'indestructible'
akshara); 'life' or 'vital air' *(prána)*; 'who,' 'who'? 'he,' 'this.'

Thus have the twenty-five 'principles' *(tatwa)* been explained
—viz :, the eight 'producers' [No. 5], the sixteen 'productions'
[No. 26], and 'soul' [No. 34].

"He who knows the twenty-five principles, whatever order of
life he may have entered, and whether he wear matted hair, a
top-knot only, or be shaven, he is liberated:—of this there is
no doubt."

अथाह । पुरुषः किं कर्त्ता अकर्त्तेति । यदि कर्त्ता पुरुषः
स्यात् शुभान् कुर्य्यात् नतु वृत्तित्रयं ।

No. 38.—Here it is asked—is 'soul' an agent, or not an agent ?
If 'soul' were an agent, it would do only good actions—it would
not adopt the 'triad of habits.'

[What the three 'habits' are, is next stated.]

धर्माख्यं शौचित्यं यमनियमनिर्वैरिणं प्रसंख्यानं ज्ञानैश्वर्य्यप्रका-
शनमिति सात्विकी वृत्तिः ।

No. 39.—The 'amiable' *(sátwika)* habit consists of virtue,

No. 41.—Madness, intoxication, lassitude, atheism, addiction to women, drowsiness, sloth, worthlessness, impurity—this is called the ' dark' (*támasa*) habit.

एतद् वृत्तिचयं दृष्टा लोके गुणानां कर्तृत्वं सिद्धमितिचाकर्त्ता पुरुषः सिद्धो भवति ।

No. 42.—Since we see this triad of habits in the world, the agency of the ' qualities' [in which these habits originate—see No. 49] is established ; and hence ' soul' [the agency being thus accounted for independently of it] is proved to be ' not an agent.'

इमान्गुणान्प्रकृतेर्वर्त्तमानान् रजस्तमोभ्यां। विपरीतदर्शनात् । अहं करोमीत्यबुधो ऽभिमन्यते । ग्रहस्य कुब्जीकरणे ऽप्यनीश्वरः सर्वमिदं मया कृतं ममेदं इतिवदन्नभिमानादबुध उन्मत्तः कर्तृ-वद्भवति ।

No. 43.—Through ' passion' (No. 51) and ' darkness' (No.

52), through an erroneous view, it (viz., 'soul') foolishly imagines—'I am the agent' in regard to these 'qualities' (No. 49) which belong to nature. Though incompetent even to the crooking of a straw, ('soul' imagines) 'All this was made by me—this is mine :'—thus saying, it, through a vain imagination, foolish, insane, becomes as if it were an agent.

अचाह ॥ प्रकृते: क्रियमाणानि गुणै: कर्माणि भागश: ।

अहंकारविमूढात्मा कर्त्ताहमिति मन्यते ॥

अनादित्वान्निर्गुणत्वात्परमात्मायमव्यय: ।

शरीरस्थोऽपि कौन्तेय न करोति न लिप्यते ॥

एवं ॥ प्रकृत्यैवच कर्माणि क्रियमाणानि सर्वश: ।

य: पश्यति तयात्मानमकर्त्तारं स पश्यति ॥

No. 44.—On this subject it is said (in the *Bhagavad Gítá*—Lect. III v. 27.) " Actions are effected by the qualities of nature, according to their shares :—the soul, deluded by the conceit of individuality, imagines 'I am the agent.'"

(And again, Lect. XIII. v. 31.)

" From its being without beginning, and its being devoid of the ' qualities,' this incorruptible supreme Soul, even while remaining in body, neither acts nor is affected."

Also—(Lect. XIII. v. 29).

" Whoso beholds actions as in all respects performed by nature alone, and so too beholds Soul as a non-agent—he indeed sees (aright)."

तच्चाह । किमयमेक: पुरुषो बहवो वेत्युच्यते । सुखदु:खमोह-संकरविमुक्तकरणपाटवजन्ममरणकरणानां नानात्वात्पुरुषबहुत्वं सिद्धं लोकाश्रमवर्णभेदाच्च । यद्येक: पुरुष: स्यादेकस्मिन् सुखिनि

सर्व एव सुखिनः स्युः । एकस्मिन् दुःखिनि सर्व एव दुःखिनः स्युः । एकस्मिन् मूढे सर्व मूढाः स्युः । एकस्मिन् संकीर्णे सर्व सं-कीर्णाः स्युः । एकस्मिन् विशुद्धे सर्व विशुद्धाः स्युः । एकस्मिन् करणपाटवे सर्वेषां करणपाटवं स्यात् । एकस्मिन् जाते सर्व जा-येरन् । एकस्मिन् मृते सर्व म्रियेरन् । इति नचैक इतश्च बहवः पुरुषाः सिद्धाः । आकृतिगर्भाश्रयभागसंगतिविभागलिंगबहुत्वात् ।

No. 45.—Here the question occurs—is 'soul' one, or many? To this it is replied:—the multiplicity of ' soul' is proved by the diversity of the conditions of pleasure, pain, delusion, mixture of race, purity of race, soundness of organs, birth, and death, and by the difference of the world (heaven, earth, and hell,) and of office, and of caste. If there were only one ' soul,' then, when one is happy, all would be happy; when one is grieved, all would be grieved; when one is deluded, all would be deluded; when one is of mixed race, all would be of mixed race; when one is of pure race, all would be of pure race; when one possesses soundness of organs, all would possess soundness of organs; when one is born, all would be born; when one dies, all would die. Hence 'soul' is not one; and hence multifarious 'souls' are proved to exist—for these possess a multiplicity of distinctive characters in the diversified allotment of form, birth, habitation, fortune, society, and body.

एवं तावत्सांख्याचार्याः कपिलासुरिपञ्चशिखपतञ्जलिप्रभृतयो बहुन्पुरुषान्वर्णयन्ति । वेदान्तवादिन आचार्या हरिहरहिरण्यगर्भ-व्यासादय एकमेवात्मानं वर्णयन्ति ।

No. 46.—Thus [as set forth in No. 45] do the teachers of the

Sánkhya, Kapila, Asuri, Panchas'ikha, Patanjali, &c., describe souls as many. The teachers who speak according to the *Vedánta* [the doctrine derived from the *Vedas*,] viz., Harihara, Hiranya-garbha, Vyása, &c., describe Soul as one only.

कस्मादेवं । तदाह । पुरुष एवेदं । सर्व्वं यद्भूतं यच्च भाव्यं उता-मृतत्वस्येशानो यदन्येनातिरोहति । तदेवाग्निस्तदादित्यस्तद्वा-युस्तच्च चन्द्रमाः । तदेव शुक्रं तद्ब्रह्म तदापः स प्रजापतिः । तदेव सत्यममृतं स नोच्चः सा परागतिः । तदद्वरं तत्सवितुर्व्वरेण्यं यस्मा-त्परं नापरमस्ति किञ्चित् यस्मान्नाणीयो न ज्यायो ऽस्ति किञ्चित् ।

No. 47.—Why thus (but one)? He replies. This [universe] is Soul only. [Soul is] all that has been, and that is to be, and the lord of immortality—that which by nought else is overlaid. It alone is fire, it is the sun, it is air, and it is the moon. It alone is pure, it is the vast one, it is the waters, it is the lord of creatures, it alone is the true nectar of immortality, it is liberation, it is the ultimate goal, it is the indestructible, it is the glory of the sun, it is that beyond which there is nothing else, than which there is nothing either more recent or more ancient.

यच्च इव स्तब्धो दिवि तिष्ठत्येकस्तेनेदं पूर्णं पुरुषेण सर्व्वं सर्व्वतः पाणिपादं तत्सर्व्वतोच्चिशिरोमुखं सर्व्वतः श्रुतिमल्लोके सर्व्वमावृत्य तिष्ठति । सर्व्वेन्द्रियगुणाभासं सर्व्वेन्द्रियविवर्जितं । सर्व्वेषां प्रभु-मीशानं सर्व्वस्य शरणं महत् । सर्व्वतः सर्व्वतत्त्वानि सर्व्वात्मा सर्व्व-सम्भवः । सर्व्वं निलीयते यस्मिन् तद्ब्रह्म मुनयो विदुः । एक एव हि भूतात्मा देहे देहे व्यवस्थितः । एकधा बहुधा चैव दृश्य-

No. 48.—Firm as a tree it remains in the heavens. With that
Soul all this is filled everywhere. On all sides are the hands,
feet, eyes, heads, and faces of that [Soul-tree]—and, with ears
in all directions, it stands embracing all—assuming the aspect of
all the organs and qualities, though devoid of all the qualities—
the lord and ruler of all—the great refuge of all—that which al-
together is all the principles, is every soul, is the source of all—
into which all is resolved—the sages regard it as *Brahma*. For
only one soul is located in various bodies ; as the Moon, though
but one, appears many in [many vessels of] water. In all existences, immoveable or locomotive, it dwells—one only—by which
all this [universe] was spread out. This soul, of all worlds, is
but one :—by *whom* is it made more ? Some speak of soul
as several—seeing that Knowledge and other mental states are ob-
servable [simultaneously—some being happy while others are sad];
but in the Bráhman, the worm, and the insect ; in the outcaste,
the dog, and the elephant ; in goats, cows, gadflies, and gnats,
the wise behold the same [single Soul]. Just as a thread may
pass through golden beads, and again in like manner through
pearls, gems, coral, earthen beads, or silver,—so this Soul is to be

regarded as remaining everywhere one—in cows, men, elephants, deer, &c.

अचाह किं त्रैगुख्यं नाम । उच्यते । सत्त्वरजस्तमांसीति त्रैगुख्यं । त्रिगुणा एव त्रैगुख्यं ।

No. 49.—Now it is asked—what is the ' triad of qualities'? It is replied—the triad of qualities consists of ' Goodness' (*sattwa*), ' Foulness' (*rajas*), and ' Darkness' (*tamas*). By the ' triad of qualities' is meant the ' three qualities.'

सत्त्वं नाम प्रसादलाघवप्रसन्नाभीष्टगतितुष्टितितिक्षासन्तोषादि लक्षणमनन्तभेदं समासतसुखात्मकं ।

No. 50.—' Goodness' (*sattwa*) is endlessly diversified, accordingly as it is exemplified in calmness, lightness, complacency, attainment of wishes, kindliness, contentment, patience, joy, and the like. Summarily, it consists of happiness.

रजो नाम शोकतापभेदेर्ईगदोषगमनादिलक्षणमनन्तभेदं समासतो दुःखात्मकं ।

No. 51.—' Foulness' (*rajas*) is endlessly diversified, accordingly as it is exemplified in grief, distress, separation, excitement, anxiety, fault-finding, and the like. Summarily, it consists of pain.

तमो नाम आच्छादनाज्ञानबीभत्सदैन्यगौरवालस्यनिद्राप्रमादादिलक्षणमनन्तभेदं समासतो मोहात्मकं ।

No. 52.—' Darkness' (*tamas*) is endlessly diversified, accordingly as it it is exemplified in envelopement, ignorance, disgust, abject-ness, heaviness, sloth, drowsiness, intoxication, and the like.

अचाह कः संचरः प्रतिसंचरस्व । अचोच्यते । उत्पत्तिः संच-
रः । प्रलयः प्रतिसंचरः । तचोत्पत्तिर्नाम ।

अव्यक्तात्प्रागुपदिष्टात्सर्वगतपुरुषेण परेणाधिष्ठिता बुद्धि रुत्य-
द्यते । अष्टगुणा बुद्धिः । बुद्धेस्तत्वादहंकार उत्पद्यते । सो ऽहंकार-
स्त्रिविधो वैकारिकस्तैजसो भूतादिरिति । तच वैकारिकादहंकाराद्
देवता इन्द्रियाणिचोत्पद्यन्ते । भूतादेस्तन्माचाणि । तैजसादुभ-
यं । तन्माचेभ्यो भूतानीति संचरः ।

No. 54.—The next question is—what is (meant by) 'developement'
and 'resolution' *(sanchara* and *pratisanchara*—the 5th and 6th in
Kapila's enumeration of topics—No. 6)? To this it is replied—
'development' is production :—' reabsorption' (*pratisanchara*)
is dissolution. [The order of] 'production' is as follows :—
from the ' undiscrete' beforementioned [No. 7], superintended by
Soul, which is another [than Nature, and for whose use is the
assemblage of sensible objects,] and omnipresent, 'intellect' is

produced. 'Intellect' is of eight kinds—[No. 9]. From the principle of 'intellect' 'self-consciousness' [No. 17] is produced. 'Self-consciousness' is of three kinds [No. 18]—the 'modifying,' the 'active,' 'ardent,' or 'urgent,' and the 'origin of the elements.' From the 'modifying self-consciousness' the gods and the senses are produced; from [self-consciousness as] 'the origin of the elements' the 'subtile elements' (No. 19) are produced. From the 'active' both proceed, [for, without the 'active,' both the others are held to be inert]. From the 'subtile elements [are produced] the [gross] 'elements :'—such is [the order of] 'development.'

प्रतिसंचरो नाम भूतानि तन्माचेषु लीयन्ते तन्माचाणीन्द्रिया-
णिचाहंकारे ऽहंकारो बुद्धौ बुद्धिरव्यक्ते । तद्व्यक्तं क्वचिन्न प्रली-
यते । कस्मादनुत्पद्यमानत्वात् । प्रकृतिं पुरुषंचैव विज्ञानादीत्ये-
वं प्रतिसंचरो व्याख्यातः ।

No. 55.—'Reabsorption' [No. 6] is as follows :—the 'elements' are resolved into the 'subtile elements ;' the 'subtile elements' and the 'senses' into 'self-consciousness ;' 'self-consciousness' into 'intellect ;' 'intellect' into the 'undiscrete.' The 'undiscrete' is nowhere dissolved. Why? Because it was not produced out of anything (into which it might be resolvable). Regard Nature and Soul as being both eternal. Thus has 'reabsorption' been explained.

तच्चाच किं तदध्यात्ममधिभूतमधिदैवंचेति । तचोच्यते । बु-
द्धिरध्यात्मं बोधयितव्यमधिभूतं ब्रह्मा तचाधिदैवतं । अहंकारो
ऽध्यात्मं मन्तव्यमधिभूतं रुद्रस्तचाधिदैवतं । मनोऽध्यात्मं संकल्पि-

तव्यमधिभूतं चन्द्रस्तचाधिदैवतं । श्रोत्रमध्यात्मं श्रोतव्यमधिभूतं
आकाशमधिदैवतं । त्वगध्यात्मं स्पर्शयितव्यमधिभूतं वायुस्तचाधि-
दैवतं । चक्षुरध्यात्मं द्रष्टव्यमधिभूतं आदित्यस्तचाधिदैवतं ।
जिह्वाध्यात्मं रसयितव्यमधिभूतं वरुणस्तचाधिदैवतं । घ्राणमध्या-
त्मं घ्रातव्यमधिभूतं पृथ्वी तचाधिदैवतं । वागध्यात्मं वक्तव्यमधि-
भूतं वह्निस्तचाधिदैवतं पाणी अध्यात्मं ग्रहीतव्यमधिभूतं इन्द्रस्त-
चाधिदैवतं । पादावध्यात्मं गन्तव्यमधिभूतं विष्णुस्तचाधिदैव-
तं । पायुरध्यात्मं उत्स्रष्टव्यमधिभूतं मित्रस्तचाधिदैवतं । उपस्थ-
मध्यात्मं आनन्दयितव्यमधिभूतं प्रजापतिस्तचाधिदैवतं । एवमेतत्त्व-
योदशविधस्य करणस्याध्यात्ममधिभूतमधिदैवतं ।

No. 56.—Now it is asked—what is meant by the 'ministers
of soul' [No 6], the 'province of an organ,' and the 'presiding
deity?' To this it is replied:—'intellect' is a 'minister of soul;'
'whatever is to be understood' constitutes its 'province;' and its
'presiding deity' is Brahmá. 'Self-consciousness' is a 'minister
of soul;' whatever is 'to be believed' constitutes its 'province;'
and Rudra is its 'presiding deity.' 'Mind' is a 'minister of soul;'
whatever is 'to be resolved on' constitutes its 'province;' the
Moon is its 'presiding deity.' The 'hearing' is a 'minister of
soul;' whatever is 'to be heard' constitutes its 'province;' the
Ether is its 'supernatural presiding power.' The 'touch' is a
'minister of soul;' whatever is 'to be touched' constitutes its
'province;' the air is its 'supernatural presiding power.' The
'sight' is a 'minister of soul;' whatever is 'to be seen' constitutes its 'province;' the sun is its 'presiding deity.' The

'taste' is a 'minister of soul;' whatever is 'to be tasted' constitutes its 'province;' Varuna [the god of the waters] is its 'presiding deity.' The 'smell' is a 'minister of soul;' whatever is 'to be smelled' constitutes its 'province;' the Earth is its 'supernatural presiding power.' The 'voice' is a 'minister of soul;' whatever is 'to be uttered' constitutes its 'province;' its 'presiding deity' is either Saraswatí or Fire. The 'hands' are 'ministers of soul;' whatever is 'to be grasped' constitutes their 'province;' Indra is their 'presiding deity'. The feet are 'ministers of soul;' whatever is 'to be gone over' constitutes their 'province;' Vishnu is their 'presiding deity.' The 'organ of excretion' is a 'minister of soul;' whatever is 'to be excreted' constitutes its 'province;' Mitra is its 'presiding deity'. The 'organ of generation' is a 'minister of soul;' what is 'to be enjoyed' constitutes its 'province;' Prajápati is its 'presiding deity.'

Such, in the case of each of the thirteen kinds of instruments [of the soul], is the respective 'minister,' 'province,' and 'presiding deity'.

तत्त्वानि यो वेद्यते यथावद् । गुणस्वरूपाण्यधिदैवतंच । विमुक्त-
पाप्मा गतदोषसङ्गो । गुणांस्तु भुङ्क्ते न गुणैः स युज्यते ।

॥ इति तत्त्ववादः ॥

No. 57.—Whosoever is correctly acquainted with the 'principles' [viz. the 8 'producers', 16 'productions,' and 'soul'], the nature of the 'qualities,' and the 'presiding deities' [No. 56], being liberated from his sins and released from the whole of his defects, enjoys [the various pleasing effects of] the 'qualities,' (while he remains in the world) and is liberated from the 'qualities' (when he attains to final emancipation).

येति । एवमेताः पच्चाभिबुद्वयो व्याख्याताः ।

No. 58.—Now what are those five 'intelligent functions' (No. 6)? To this it is replied:—'ascertainment' (*adhyavasáya*), 'conceit' (*abhimána*), 'willing' (*ichchhá*), 'adaptability' (*karttavyatá*), and 'action' (*kriyá*). The function of intellect when it decides 'This is to be done by me,' is 'ascertainment' (*adhyavasáya*). That function of the intellect, self-consciousness,—the notion that 'I act'—which fixes on the conceptions of 'self' and 'not-self'—is 'conceit'. The intelligent function of 'mind' is 'willing'—desiring and purposing. The intelligent function of the organs of sense (No. 27) is the 'adaptability' of each sense, such as the hearing, or the like, to its object, such as sound, or the like. The intelligent function of those (organs of action—No. 29—) which are recognised by 'utterance,' and the like, is called 'action'.

Thus have the five 'intelligent functions' been explained.

अथ काष्ठाः पच्च कर्म्मयोनय इत्युच्यते । धृतिः श्रद्धा सुखा
ऽविविदिषा विविदिषाच पच्च कर्म्मयोनयः ।

वाच्यकर्म्माणि संकल्प्य प्रतीतं योऽभिरच्चति ।

तन्निष्ठत्वप्रतिष्ठत्व धृतेरेतद्धि लच्चणं ॥

स्वाध्यायो ब्रह्मचर्यञ्च यजनं याजनं तपः ।

दानं प्रतिग्रहो होमः श्रद्धाया लच्चणं स्मृतं ॥

सुखार्थं वस्तु सेवेत विद्याकर्म्मतपांसिच ।

प्रायश्चित्तपरो नित्यं सुखेयं परिकीर्त्तिता ॥

विषयभधुमिश्रितान्तः करणत्वमविविदिषा । विविदिषाच ध्या-

निनां प्रज्ञानयोनिः ।

एकत्वंच पृथत्तंच नित्वंचैवमचेतनं ।

सूच्मसत्कार्यमच्छोभ्यं ज्ञेया विविदिषाच सा ॥

कार्य्यकारणच्वयकरी विविदिषा प्राकृतिकी वृत्तिः ।

एवमेताः पंच कर्म्मयोनयो व्याख्याताः ।

No. 59.—Now, what are those five 'sources of action' (No. 6) ?
To this it is replied :—'firmness,' or 'decision of character'
(*dhriti*), 'faith' (*s'raddhá*), 'piety' (*sukhá*), 'indifference about
knowledge' (*avividishá*), and 'desire of knowledge' (*vividishá*) :
—these are the five 'sources of action.'

Having resolved on any outward act, he who keeps his pur-
pose, being intent on it, and carrying it into effect,—this [con-
duct of such a man] furnishes the definition of 'firmness.'

The characters by which 'faith' may be recognised are stated
to be the perusal of the Scriptures, the condition of the religious
student, sacrificing or causing sacrifices, penance, giving and re-
ceiving proper donations, and making oblations.

But he who may addict himself to study, to religious actions,
and austerities, being always intent on penances with a view to the

see No. 69)—this is to be considered (as constituting the assemblage of matters which form the object of) 'the desire of (true) knowledge'.

अथाथ के पञ्च वायवः । उच्यते । प्राणो ऽपानः समानश्च उदानो व्यान एवच इत्येते वायवः पञ्च शरीरेषु शरीरिणां । तच्च प्राणो नाम वायुर्मुखनासिकाधिष्ठाता प्रणयनात्प्रक्रमणाच्च प्राण इत्यभिधीयते । अपानो नाम वायुर्नाभ्यधिष्ठाता अपनयनादा धोगमनाच्चापान इत्यभिधीयते । समानो नाम वायुर्हृदधिष्ठाता समनयनात्समगमनाच्च समान इत्यभिधीयते । उदानो नाम वायुः कण्ठाधिष्ठाता ऊर्द्धगमनादुत्क्रमणाचोदान इत्यभिधीयते । व्यानः सर्वव्यापकः । इति पञ्च वायवो व्याख्याताः ।

No. 60.—It is now asked—what are the five 'airs' (No. 6)? To this it is replied :—the five airs, in the bodies of those who have bodies, are those named *prána, apána, samána, udána*, and *vyána*. The 'air' called *prána* is that which is superintended by the mouth and nose. It is so named because it comprises 'inspiration' (*pranayana*) and 'expiration' (*prakramana*). [This refers to

the process of *respiration*]. The 'air' called *apána* is that which
is superintended by the navel. It is so called from its 'taking
away' (*apanayana*), and 'going downwards'. [This refers to
flatulence]. The 'air' called *samána* is superintended by the
heart. It is so called from its 'leading and going equably'
[neither up nor down—as far as regards the food, to aid in the
digestion of which is its province]. The 'air' called *udána* is that
which is superintended by the throat. It is so named from its
ascending and 'going upwards' (*utkramana*). [This refers to the
arterial pulsation &c. of the upper members of the body—the throat
and head]. The 'air' called *vyána* is the 'pervader' (*vyápaka*)
of the whole body. [This refers to pulsation in general and all
the other involuntary actions of the system.]

Thus have the five 'airs' been described.

अथाह के ते पञ्च कर्म्मात्मान इत्युच्यते । वैकारिकस्तैजसो
भूतादिः सानुमानो निरनुमानश्च । तच वैकारिकः शुभकर्म्मकर्त्ता ।
तैजसो ऽशुभकर्म्मकर्त्ता । भूतादिनिंगूढकर्मकर्त्ता । सानुमानः शुभ-
मूढकर्त्ता । निरनुमानो ऽशुभमूढकर्त्ताचैव पञ्च कर्मात्मानो व्या-
ख्याताः ।

No. 61.—It is now asked—what are those five 'whose nature is
action' (No. 6)? To this it is replied:—the 'modifying' (*vaikárika*), the 'ardent' (*taijasa*), the 'origin of the elements' (*bhútádi*),
that which is 'associated with inference' (*sánumána*), and that which
is 'not associated with inference' (*niranumána*). Among these
the 'modifying' [form of 'self-consciousness'—see No. 18—] is
the agent in good actions:—the 'ardent' is the agent in actions
not good:—the 'origin of the elements' is the producer of things
good but obscure:—[self-consciousness] 'associated with inference'
is the worker of what is good but foolish:—and that which is 'not

मोहो दशात्मकः । तामिस्रोऽन्धतामिस्रश्चाष्टादशात्मकौ । तमो नामाष्टसु प्रकृतिव्यक्तबुद्ध्यहंकारपंचतन्मात्रसंज्ञितासु अनात्मसु आत्माभिमानस्त्वम इत्यभिधीयते । मोहो नाम अणिमाद्यैश्वर्यं प्राप्यं यो ऽभिमान उत्पद्यते स मोह इत्यभिधीयते । महामोहो नाम दृष्टानुश्रविकेषु शब्दादिविषयेषु दशसु वृत्तिषु मुक्तो ऽह-मिति मन्यते स महामोह इत्यभिधीयते । तामिस्रो नामाष्टगुणै-श्वर्येऽणिमाद्ये दशविधेच विषये यो द्वेषो ऽप्रतिघातस्त्वयं दुःखमु-त्पद्यते ऽसौ तामिस्र इत्यभिधीयते । अन्धतामिस्रो नामाष्टगुणैश्वर्येऽणिमाद्ये दशविधेच विषये सिद्धे मरणकाले यो विषाद उत्पद्यते सो ऽन्धतामिस्र इत्यभिधीयते । एवमेषा पञ्चपर्वा ऽविद्या द्विष्टिभेदाऽऽख्याता ।

No. 62.—Here it is asked—what is that 'ignorance'—under five divisions [No. 6] ? To this it is replied :—'obscurity' (*tamas*), 'illusion' (*moha*), 'extreme illusion' (*mahámoha*), 'gloom' (*támisra*), and 'utter darkness' (*andha-támisra*). Among these, 'obscurity' and 'illusion' are each eightfold. 'Extreme illusion' is tenfold. 'Gloom' and 'utter darkness' are eighteenfold.

'Obscurity' is the conceit that [he will be liberated from transmigration because] soul [merges] into [some one or other of] the eight 'producers,' which are not Soul—viz., those called the 'undiscrete,' 'intellect,' 'self-consciousness,' and the five 'subtile 'elements,'—[the errors in regard to these eight severally making up the eight varieties of 'obscurity']. 'Illusion' is the conceit (of liberation) which arises from the possession of the eight kinds of superhuman power, such as 'minuteness' and the rest (No. 13). 'Extreme illusion' is when one supposes 'I am liberated' through (any one of) the ten modes (supplied by) the objects of sense, viz., sounds, &c., belonging to the seen and to the unseen (or scripture-revealed) world—(i. e. the five as perceived by men and the five as perceived by the gods). 'Gloom' is that unchecked hate (or fierce impatience) in regard to the (possession of the) eight kinds of superhuman power, 'minuteness,' &c., and the ten kinds of objects of sense, which (by preventing liberation) results in the three kinds of pain (incident to corporeal existence.) 'Utter darkness' is the name given to that grief which arises at the time of death, when one is in possession of (any one of) the eight kinds of super-human power, or of the ten kinds of objects of sense.

Thus has fivefold 'ignorance' (the obstruction to the soul's object of final liberation) in its sixty-two varieties, been declared.

अचाद्ध का सा अष्टविंशतिधा ऽशक्तिरुच्यते । एकादशेन्द्रिय-
बधाः सप्तदश बुद्धिबधाः । एषाष्टविंशतिधा ऽशक्तिरिति । तचे-
न्द्रियबधास्तावदुच्यन्ते । श्रोत्रे बाधिर्यं जिह्वायांजडत्वं त्वचि कु-
ष्ठितं चच्षूरूपत्वं नासिकायामघ्राणत्वं वाचि मूकत्वं हस्तयोः कु-
ष्ठितं पादयोः पंगुत्वं पायिन्द्रिये उदावर्त उपस्थेन्द्रिये क्लैब्यं
मनसि उन्माद इत्येकादशेन्द्रियबधाः । सप्तदशबुद्धिबधा नाम वि-
पर्ययात्तुष्टिसिड्डीनां । तुष्टिविपर्ययास्तावदुच्यन्ते ।

No. 63.—It is now asked—what is twenty-eightfold 'disability' (No. 6)? To this it is replied:—the depravity of the eleven organs, and the seventeen injuries of the intellect—these constitute twenty-eightfold 'disability.' Now the defects of the organs are stated:—in the organ of hearing, deafness; in the organ of taste, insensibility; in the organ of touch, leprosy; in the organ of sight, blindness; in the organ of smell, loss of smell; in the organ of utterance, dumbness; in the hands, crippledness; in the feet, lameness; in the organ of excretion, constipation; in the organ of generation, impotence; in the mind, insanity:—such are the defects of the eleven organs. The seventeen 'injuries of the intellect' are the reverse of (the nine kinds of) 'acquiescence' and of (the eight kinds of) 'perfectness.' What is meant by the 'reverse of acquiescence' is next stated.

तच्च नास्ति प्रधानमिति या प्रतिपत्तिरनन्ता । एवं महत्त्या-त्मज्ञाने तामसलीना । तथाहंकारस्यादर्शनमवेद्या । नैव सन्ति तन्मात्राणि भूतकारणानीत्यदृष्टि: । विषयाणामर्जने प्रवृत्तिरसु-तारा । रक्षणे तु प्रवृत्तिरसुपाराच । स्वयदोषमदृष्ट्वार्थेषु प्रवृत्ति-रसुनेचा । भोगासक्तिरसुमरीचिका । हिंसादोषमपश्यतो भो-गारम्भो ऽनुत्तमाम्भसिका । इति तुष्टिविपर्यया नवधा ऽतुष्टयो व्याख्याता: ।

No. 64.—Among these [that are the 'reverse of acquiescence' —No. 66—] that called *anantá* is the belief that there is no such thing as Nature. In like manner, (non-acquiescence) in the notion that Soul consists of Intellect, is that called *támasa-líná*. So, again—the non-recognition of 'self-consciousness' is that called *avedyá*. (The notion that) there are no 'subtile elements,' the causes of the gross elements, is that called *avrishti*. The concerning one's self about the acquisition of the objects of sense is that (form of non-acquiescence) called *asutára ;* and (the concerning one's self) about their preservation is that called *asupára.* The concerning one's self about property, without regarding the evils of waste, is that called *asunetra.* The addiction to enjoyment is that called *asumaríchiká.* The engaging in enjoyment, on the part of one who does not look to the evils arising from injury (to created beings), is that called *anuttamámbhasiká.*

Thus have the ninefold opposites of acquiescence been explained.

[The technical names here are the opposites of those adverted to in section No. 66.]

अथ सिद्धिविपर्ययाः । असिद्धयो ऽष्टावाचाभिधीयन्ते । नानात्वं भूतमाचष्टे कल्वमाविभूतमतारमुच्यते । शब्दमाचश्रवणादिपरीतग्रहणमसुतारं । यथा नानात्वन्नो मुक्त इति श्रुत्वा विपरीतं प्रतिपन्नो नानात्वन्नो ह्यमुक्त इति । अध्ययनश्रवणाभिनिविष्टस्यापि जडत्वादसच्छास्त्रोपहतबुद्धित्वाद्वा पञ्चविंशतितत्त्वज्ञानसिद्धिर्न भवति तदा ऽतारतारं तज्ज्ञानं । कस्यचिदाध्यात्मिकेन दुःखेनाभिभूतस्यापि संसारेऽनुद्वेगादजिज्ञासोर्न ज्ञानं प्रमोदं । एवमप्रमुदिताप्रमोदमानयोश्वान्योन्ययोर्द्वयमपरं द्रष्टव्यं । सुहृदुपदिष्टे ऽप्यनिश्चयबुद्धेरज्ञानमरसं । असम्यग्वचनाद्यथवा पराङ्मुखे गुरौ दुर्भाग्यस्य ज्ञानासिद्धिस्तदज्ञानमसत्प्रमुदितमिति । एवमेते सिद्धिविपर्यया असिद्धयो ऽष्टौ व्याख्याताः । एवमेषास्ताविंशतिधा ऽशक्तिराख्याता ।

No. 65.—Now (as regards) the 'opposites' of perfectness. These are called also the eight 'imperfections' (*asiddhi*). When the diversity (of the various principles from which the creation proceeds) appears as the unity of the mere (phenomenal) creation —this (imperfect view of the truth) is called *atára*. After hearing the words merely (of a competent instructor), the adoption of the contrary is that called *asutára* :—as when, having heard that 'he who acknowledges the various principles is liberated,' one determines that it is the reverse—viz., that 'he who acknowledges the various principles is *not* liberated.' When a person, even though intent on studying and hearing, through obtuseness or from his intellect's being impaired by unsound doctrine, does not attain to a perfect knowledge of the twenty-five principles, then his ignorance is called *atáratára*. To another, who, though oppressed by the pain inseparable from body and mind, yet, from feeling no anxiety about transmigration, entertains no curiosity, knowledge is no 'delight' (*pramoda*). Analogously are the next two to be regarded —viz., (the forms of 'imperfection' termed—as the opposites of the corresponding two forms of 'perfectness' in No. 67—) *apramudita* and *apramodamána*. Ignorance that arises from the not arriving at certain knowledge even on being instructed by a friend, is that called *arasya*. When, from his preceptor's disregarding him, or not instructing him correctly, an unfortunate man does not attain to knowledge, his ignorance is called *asatpramudita*.

Thus have those 'opposites of perfectness,' the eight imperfections, been explained. [The technical names are the opposites of those adverted to in section No. 67.]

Thus have the twenty-eight kinds of 'disability' [No. 63] been explained.

अथाह का सा नवधा तुष्टिरुच्योच्यते । प्रकृतिं परमात्मत्वेन

परिकल्प्य परितुष्ये माध्यस्थ्यं लभते तस्य तुष्टेर्या सा ताम्बि-
कीसंज्ञात्रम्भ इति। अपरो बुद्धिं परमात्मत्वेन प्रतिपद्य परितुष्टस्य
तुष्टे: सलिला इति संज्ञा। अन्यो ऽहंकारं परमात्मत्वेनाभ्युपगम्य प-
रितुष्टस्य तुष्टेरोघ इति संज्ञा। इतरत्तन्माचापि अभोग्याख्यानि
परमात्मत्वेन विनिश्चित्य परितुष्टस्य तुष्ट: वृष्टिरिति संज्ञा।
एवं अध्यात्मिकास्ततष्टयो भवन्ति। चतसृष्वपि तुष्टिषु ना-
स्ति मोचत्तत्वज्ञानस्यासम्भवात्। बाह्या अर्थार्जनरच्चणव्ययसंग
हिंसादिदोषदर्शनाद्विषयोपरमे पञ्च तुष्टयो भवन्ति। अर्थाना-
र्जने दोषदर्शनात्तुष्ट: प्रव्रजितस्यापि नास्ति मोचत्तत्वज्ञानाभा-
वात् सा पञ्चमी तुष्टि: सुतारेत्यभिधीयते। अन्यो ऽर्यानां रच्चणे
दोषदर्शनात्तुष्ट: प्रव्रजितस्यापि नास्ति मोचत्तत्त्वज्ञानाभावात् सा
षष्टी तुष्टि: सुपारेत्युच्यते। अन्यो ऽर्यानां च्चये दोषदर्शनात्तुष्ट: प्रव्र-
जित स्यापि नास्ति मोचत्तत्वज्ञानाभावात् सा सप्तमी तृष्टि: सुने-
चेत्यभिधीयते। अन्यो ऽर्यानां संगदोषदर्शनान्निवृत्तस्तुष्ट: प्रव्रजित-
स्यापि नास्ति मोचत्तत्वज्ञानाभावात् सा ऽष्टमी तुष्टि: सुमरीचि-
कोत्यभिधीयते। अन्यो भूतानामर्थनिमित्तहिंसादिदोषदर्शनान्निवृ-
त्तस्तुष्ट: प्रव्रजितस्यापि नास्ति मोचत्तत्वज्ञानाभावात् सा नवमी
तुष्टिरुत्तमा सात्विकीत्यभिधीयते। इत्येता नव तुष्टयो व्याख्याताः।

No. 66.—Now it is asked—what is ninefold 'acquiescence'
[No. 6]? To this it is replied :—having supposed that Nature is
Soul, a man contentedly betakes himself to indifference :—the

come to the conclusion that 'self-consciousness' is Soul, is contented. The technical name of his 'acquiescence' is *ogha* 'quantity.' Another, having decided that the 'subtile elements,' those called the 'unfitted for [mortal] fruition' [No. 25] are Soul, is contented. The technical name of his 'acquiescence' is *vrishti* 'rain.' Such are the four 'internal' or 'spiritual' (*ádhyátmika*) kinds of 'acquiescence.' Where [together or separately] those four kinds of acquiescence exist, liberation does not take place—from the inconsistency [of such sentiments] with a knowledge of the principles.

The five 'external' (*váhya*) kinds of 'acquiescence' consist in abstaining from [the enjoyment of the five] objects of sense, [such abstinence proceeding] from observation of the evils of acquiring, preserving, waste, attachment [to sensual pleasures], and injuriousness. A man is acquiescent (and abstinent) from observation of the evils attendant on the acquiring of property; but his liberation—even though he be an ascetic—does not take place, because of the (quite possibly concurrent, and here assumed,) absence of a knowledge of the principles. This fifth kind of 'acquiescence' is (technically) named *sutára*. Another is acquiescent from observation of the evils attendant on the preserving of property; but his liberation—even though he be an ascetic—in the absence of a knowledge of the principles, does not take place. This sixth kind of 'acquiescence' is (technically) named *supárá*. Another is acquiescent from observation of the evils of the waste of property; but his liberation—even though he be an ascetic—in the absence of a knowledge of the principles, does not take place. This seventh kind of 'acquiescence' is (technically) named *sunetra* ('a beautiful eye'). Another is acquiescent from observation of the evils attendant on attachment (to sensual pleasures)—but his liberation—even though he be an ascetic—in the absence of a knowledge of the principles, does not take place. This eighth kind of 'acquiescence' is (technically) named *sumaríchiká*. Another is acquiescent, and abstains from worldly acts, from observation of the evils in the shape of injury, &c., to created beings on account of property—but his liberation—even though he be an ascetic—in the absence of a knowledge of the principles, does not take place. This ninth kind of 'acquiescence' is (technically) named *anuttamá* ('best'), or *sátwikí* ('amiable').

Thus have these nine kinds of acquiescence been explained.

अत्राह का ऽष्टौ सिद्धय इत्यत्रोच्यते । यदूहेन ज्ञानमुत्पद्यते तत्त्वभावभूतेषु सा प्रथमा सिद्धिस्तारेत्यभिधीयते । यच्छब्दमा- त्रेण ज्ञानमुत्पद्यते तत्त्वभावभूतेषु सा द्वितीया सिद्धिः सुतारे- त्यभिधीयते । यदध्ययनेन ज्ञानमुत्पद्यते तत्त्वभावभूतेषु सा तृ- तीया सिद्धिस्तारयन्तीत्यभिधीयते। यदाध्यात्मिकस्य दुःखस्याप- नोदनं कृत्वा ज्ञानमुत्पद्यते तत्त्वभावभूतेषु सा चतुर्थी सिद्धिः प्र- मोदेत्यभिधीयते । यदाधिभौतिकस्य दुःखस्यापनोदं कृत्वा ज्ञान- मुत्पद्यते तत्त्वभावभूतेषु सा पञ्चमी सिद्धिः प्रमोदितेत्यभिधीयते । यदाधिदैवतस्य दुःखस्यापनोदं कृत्वा ज्ञानमुत्पद्यते तत्त्वभावभूतेषु सा षष्ठी सिद्धिः प्रमोदमानेत्यभिधीयते । यत्स्निग्धसंसर्गाद्व्यपा- याज्ज्ञानमुत्पद्यते तत्त्वभावभूतेषु सा सप्तमी सिद्धिः रम्यकेत्यभिधीय-

ते । यत्परिचर्यादानेन ज्ञानमुत्पद्यते तद्भावभूतेषु परितोषिते गुरौ साष्टमी सिद्धिः सत्प्रमुदितेत्यभिधीयते । इत्येता अष्टसिद्धयो व्याख्याताः ।

No. 67.—Now it is asked—what are the eight kinds of 'perfectness' (No. 6)? To this it is replied:—the knowledge which arises from reasoning, in regard to the principles (No. 57), the conditions of intellect (No. 9), and the elemental creation (No. 72)—this, the first kind of 'perfectness,' is (technically) named *tára*. The knowledge, in regard to the principles, the conditions of intellect, and the elemental creation, which arises from hearing alone—this second kind of 'perfectness' is (technically) named *sutára*. The knowledge, in regard to the principles, the conditions of intellect, and elemental creation, which arises from study,—this third kind of 'perfectness' is (technically) named *tárayantí*. The knowledge, in regard to the principles, the conditions of intellect, and the elemental creation, which arises on effecting the removal of internal pain,—this fourth kind of 'perfectness' is (technically) named *pramoda* ('delight'). The knowledge, in regard to the principles, the conditions of intellect, and the elemental creation, which arises on effecting the removal of external pain—this fifth kind of 'perfectness' is (technically) named *pramodita* ('delighted'). The knowledge, in regard to the principles, the conditions of intellect, and the elemental creation, which arises on effecting the removal of pain occasioned by something superhuman—this sixth kind of 'perfectness' is (technically) named *pramodamána*. The knowledge, in regard to the principles, the conditions of intellect, and the elemental creation, which arises from continuance of association with amiable persons,—this seventh kind of 'perfectness' is (technically) named *ramyaká*. The knowledge, in regard

to the principles, the conditions of intellect, and the elemental
creation, when a teacher is propitiated by giving him veneration,
—this eighth kind of 'perfectness' is (technically) named *satpra-
mudita*.

Thus have these eight kinds of 'perfectness' been explained.

अचाच के दश मूलिकार्था इत्यचोच्यते । अस्तित्वमेकत्वमथार्थ-
वत्वं पराय्थमन्यत्वमकट्टत्ताच योगो वियोगो बहवः पुमांसः स्थितिः
शरीरस्य विशेषवृत्तिः । इत्येते दश मूलिकार्थाः ।

.No. 68.—Now it is asked—what are the ten 'radical facts'
(No. 6)? To this it is replied—the existence (of 'Soul' and
of 'Nature'); the singleness (of Nature); its objectiveness; its
subservience; the distinctness (of Soul from Nature); and the
inertness (of Soul); the union (of Soul and Nature); the separation (of Soul from its corporeal frame); the peculiar habit of
body—its durability (after it ought to have disappeared).

Such are the ten 'radical facts.'

संघातपरार्थत्वादिति पुरुषास्तित्वं सिद्धं। भेदानां परिमाणात्का-
रणमस्त्यव्यक्तमिति पर्यायद्वयेन प्रधानस्यास्तित्वं सिद्धं। हेतुमद्-
नित्यमित्येकत्वं सिद्धं। प्रीत्यप्रतिविषादात्मकादय इत्यर्थवत्वं
सिद्धं। नानाविधैरुपायैरिति परार्थत्वं सिद्धं। त्रिगुणमविवेकि-
विषय इत्यन्यत्वं सिद्धं। तस्माच्च विपर्ययादित्यकट्टत्वं सिद्धं।
पुरुषस्य दर्शनार्थं कैवल्यार्थं तथा प्रधानस्यापीति योगः सिद्धः।
प्राप्ते शरीरभेदे चरितार्यादिति वियोगसिद्धिः। जन्ममरणकरणा-
नामिति पुरुषबहुत्वं सिद्धं। चक्रभ्रमवदिति विशेषवृत्तिः सिद्धा।

एते दश मूलिकार्था व्याख्याताः ।

No. 69.—' Since the assemblage of sensible objects is for another's use,' the existence of Soul is established. The existence of Nature is established by the pair in order—(of antecedent and consequent)—viz., that ' since specific objects are finite,' therefore 'there is a general cause which is undiscrete'. Since 'what is causable is inconstant (and multitudinous), &c.,' the singleness (of Nature which is not caused by aught) is established. Since 'these (meaning the Qualities) consist in pleasure, pain, and dulness, &c.,' (see the XIIth of the Memorial Verses of the Sánkhya—) the objectiveness (of Nature) is established. Since 'by manifold means (Nature, without benefit to herself, accomplishes the wish of Soul,)' the subserviency (of Nature) is established. Since ' it (the ' undiscrete,' as well as its modifications) has the three qualities, is indiscriminative, objective, &c.,' the distinctness (of Soul, which is, in all these respects, the reverse,) is established. 'From the contrast' (shown to exist between active Nature and Soul) the inertness (of Soul) is established. ' For the Soul's contemplation of nature, and for its abstraction, &c.'—thus is the union (of the two) established. Since 'separation (of the Soul) from the body takes place, when the object is accomplished,' the separation of the two is established. Since ' of birth, death, and the instruments of life, (the allotment is severally diverse),' the multiplicity of Soul is established. Since it is 'like the whirling of the potter's wheel, (after the impulse that set it in motion has been discontinued),' the peculiar habit (of body, which continues, till death, to invest the soul even of him who has attained to perfect knowledge,) is established.

Thus have the ten ' radical facts' been explained.

सप्तदशानां प्रागुपदिष्टानाञ्च पञ्चास्रत प्रत्यया एतेच षष्टि

पदार्थाः षष्टितन्त्वमित्युच्यते ।

No. 70.—The fifty intellectual modifications consisting of the seventeen (enumerated in Nos. 64 and 65) and of those (thirty three) previously exhibited (in Nos. 62 and 63), together with these (ten 'radical facts'—No. 69—) make up the sixty topics called the 'System of Sixty.'

अथाच को ऽनुग्रहसर्गः । अचोच्यते । बाह्यानां पञ्चतन्मात्रेभ्यस्त्रीत्यथ्यानुग्रहसर्गः । मानोत्पत्तेराधारवज्जितानुत्पन्नान्दृष्ट्वा तेभ्यस्तन्मात्रेभ्यो ऽनुग्रहसर्गमसृजदृह्मा ।

No. 71.—Now it is asked—what is 'benevolent creation' (No. 6)? To this it is replied :—'benevolent creation' consists in the production of external objects from the five 'subtile elements.' (As it is said) ' Brahmá, perceiving these (senses, &c.) produced from thought (—see No. 19) to be destitute of a sphere of action, created, from these 'subtile elements,' this 'benevolent creation.'

अथाच कश्चतुर्दशविधो भूतसर्ग इत्यचोच्यते । अष्टविकल्पो दैवः पैशाचो राच्सो याच्यो गान्धर्व ऐन्द्रः प्राजापत्यो ब्राह्म इत्यष्टौ देवयोनयः । पञ्चधा तिर्यग्योनिश्च पशुपच्चिस्थग-चरीसृपस्थावरान्तेति । मानुष्यकञ्चैकविधं ब्राह्मणादि चाण्डालान्तं । गवादि मूषकान्तं पशवः । सिंहादि शृगालान्तं मृगाः । गरुडादि मशकान्ताः पच्चिणः । श्रेषादि कीटान्ताः सरीसृपाः । पारिजातादि तृणान्ताः स्थावराः । इति तिर्यग्योनिश्च पञ्चधा भवति । समासतो ऽयं त्रिधा सर्गः । एतत्स्वंसा-

रमण्डलमुक्तं ।

No. 72.—Now it is asked—what is the fourteenfold 'elemen_
tal creation' (No. 6) ? To this it is replied :—the divine kind is
of eight sorts—that of hobgoblins, of titans, of attendants on the
god of riches, of celestial quiristers, of demigods, of divine
sages, of the planetary regents, and of the supreme deities. Such
are the eight families of divinities. The grovelling kind is fivefold—that of domestic animals, winged animals, wild animals,
reptiles, and, lastly, of fixed things. Mankind is single in its
class—beginning with the Bráhman, and ending with the Chándála.
Domestic animals, beginning with the cow, end with the mouse.
Wild animals, beginning with the lion, end with the jackal.
Winged animals, beginning with the bird of Vishnu (or the adju-
tant), end with the gnat. Reptiles, beginning with the World-
snake, end with the worm. Fixed things, beginning with the tree
of Paradise, end with grass. Thus is the grovelling kind fivefold. Compendiously, this (elemental) creation is threefold—
(viz.,—divine, human, and grovelling—and, thus viewed, it sup-
plies the 21st topic in Kapila's enumeration—see No. 6.) All
this constitutes what is called the mundane orb.

अथाह कस्तिविधो बन्धः । इत्यचोच्यते । प्रकृतिबन्धो
वैकारिकबन्धो दचिणाबन्धस्त्रेति । तच प्रकृतिबन्धो नामाष्टौ
प्रकृतयस्ताः परत्वेनाभिमन्यमानस्य प्रकृतिलयः प्रकृतिबन्ध इत्यु-
च्यते । तच वैकारिकबन्धो नाम प्रव्रजितानां लौकिकानां वैका-
रिकेंद्रियैर्ब्रह्मदीचितानां शब्दादिविषये प्रसक्तानामजितेन्द्रियाणाम-
ज्ञानिनां काममोचितानां वैकारिकबन्ध इत्युच्यते । दचिणाबन्धो
नाम गृहस्थब्रह्मचारिभिच्चुवैखानसानां काममोहोपहतचेतसामभि-

मानपूर्विकां दच्चिणां प्रयच्छतां दच्चिणाबन्ध इत्यच्यते । इति चि-
विधो बन्धो व्याख्यातः । उत्तञ्च प्राकृतेनतु बन्धेन तथा वैकारि-
केणच । दच्चिणाभिस्तृतीयेन बन्धो ऽयच्च निगद्यते ॥

No. 73. —Now it is asked—what is threefold 'bondage' (No.
6) ? To this it is replied :—the bondage of the 'producers,' that
of the 'modifications,' and that of 'ritual observance.' And first
of the 'bondage of the producers :'—this is the name given to the
'absorption into nature' (No. 15.) of him who imagines that (any
of) the eight 'producers' constitute Soul. The 'bondage of the
modifications' is the name given to that (which opposes the liberation) of those wordly devotees who are in the power of the
'modifications' of nature (No. 26), such as the senses—who are
devoted to objects of sense, such as sounds, &c.,—who have not
their organs in subjection—who are ignorant, and deluded by
passion. The 'bondage of ritual' is the name given to that
(which opposes the liberation) of those who, whether household-
ers, students, mendicants, or anchorets, with minds vitiated by
passion and delusion, bestow (on Bráhmans, upon solemn or
sacrificial occasions,) gifts prompted by conceit.

Thus has threefold 'bondage' been explained. And it is said—
"Bondage is spoken of by the title of 'bondage through nature'—
'bondage through nature's modifications'—and, thirdly, as that
'through gifts.'"

तच्चाह कत्तिविधो मोच्चः । ज्ञानेन्द्रेकादिन्द्रियरागोपश्रमात्खत्त्व
च्चयाच्चेति। ज्ञानेन्द्रेकादिन्द्रियरागोपश्रमात्खधर्म्माधर्म्मं च्चयो भवति
धर्म्माधर्म्मच्चयाच्च कैवल्यमिति । उत्तञ्च । आत्त्याच्चि मोच्चो ज्ञानेन

senses and passions, there results the destruction both of merit and
demerit, and, from the destruction of merit and demerit, (liberation
in the shape of) ' singleness' (*kaivalya*). And it is said—" The
first liberation is (gained) by knowledge ; the second, from the
destruction of passion ; and the third, from the destruction of
all :—such are the characters of liberation."

किं चिविधं प्रमाणमित्युच्यते । दृष्टमनुमानमाप्तवचनञ्चेति । एत-
द्विविधं प्रमाणं ।

No. 75.—What is threefold ' Proof' (No. 6) ? To this it is
replied :— ' perception,' ' inference,' and ' right affirmation'—this
is threefold ' proof.'

दृष्टं तावद्व्याख्यायते । यावदिन्द्रियाणां पञ्चेन्द्रियार्थाः प्रत्यचा
एव दृष्टं ।

No. 76.—' Perception' (*drishṭa*) is now described. Whenever
the five objects of the senses are present to the senses, there is
' perception.'

अनुमानं प्रमाणं लिङ्गदर्शने जायमानं ज्ञानं । यथा मेघोदये
दृष्टिः साध्यते । बलाकादिभिः सलिलं । धूमेनाग्निः । परमिद-
मनुमानं ।

No. 77.—The proof called ' inference' is knowledge arising on the recognition of a 'sign' (*linga*). For example—by the rising of clouds (regarded as a sign of approaching rain) rain is proved (to be approaching):—by cranes and the like (regarded as a sign attendant on the sheets of water which they frequent) water (is proved to be in the neighbourhood of the place where the cranes are seen). By smoke (regarded as a sign of fire) fire (is proved to exist where the smoke originates):—this is the third kind of inference.

प्रत्यक्षेणानुमानेन वा यो ऽर्थो न साध्यते स आप्तवचनात्साध्यते ।
यथेन्द्रो देवानां राजा । उत्तराः कुरवः । सौवर्णो मेरुः । खर्गे
ऽ सरस इति । ते इन्द्रादयः प्रत्यक्षानुमानासाध्याश्च वशिष्ठादयो
मनयो वदन्ति । सन्तीन्द्रादयः । आगमो ऽप्यस्ति । खकर्म्मण्य-
भियुक्तो यो रागद्वेषविवर्जितः । ज्ञानवान् शीलसम्यन्न आप्तो हे-
यस्तु तादृशः । एवमेतत्त्रिविधं प्रमाणमभिहितं ।

No. 78.—A fact which is not established by 'perception' or by 'inference,' is established (when it is established) by 'right affirmation'. Such matters (not proveable either by perception or by inference) are (the existence of) Indra the king of the gods, the northern *Kurus*, the golden mountain *Meru*, the nymphs in Paradise. These—Indra, &c.,—not proveable either by perception or by inference, the sages, such as Vas´ishṭa declare—saying "Indra &c. *do* exist." There is also the Scripture (—which is an authority sufficient to establish such points).

"He who is assiduous in his own duties, devoid of passion and malice, intelligent, and virtuous—such a one is to be held 'worthy' (to be received as an authority in regard to matters not demonstrable by perception or by inference)."

Thus has 'threefold proof' been declared.

means of weights—so by means of this (apparatus of 'perception,'
'inference,' and 'right affirmation'), the 'principles,' the 'modifications of intellect,' and the 'elemental creation,' [—see No. 67—]
are accurately determined [*pramíyante*—whence their name of
pramána 'proof.']

चिविधेन दुःखेनाभिभूतो ब्राह्मणः कपिलमच्षि श्ररणमुपागतः ।
च्चाच किं चिविधं दुःखमित्यचोच्यते । आध्यात्मिकमाधिभौतिक-
माधिदैविकमिति ।

No. 80·—"Oppressed by 'threefold pain,' the Bráhman had
recourse to the great sage Kapila"—[see No. 5]—so the question arises—what is 'threefold pain'? To this it is replied—'natural and inseparable' (*ádhyátmika*); 'natural and extrinsic' (*ádhibhautika)*; and 'non-natural or superhuman' (*ádhidaiviká).*

तचाध्यात्मिकं द्विविधं श्ररीरं मानसच्चेति । श्ररीरे भवं श्रा-
रीरं । मनसि भवं मानसमिति । तच श्ररीरं नाम वातपित्तस्ने-
ष्मणां वैषम्याद् दुःखमुत्पद्यते । ज्वरातीसारविसूचिकामूर्च्छा-
दिकं तच्छारीरमुच्यते । कामक्रोधलोभमोहमदेर्ष्यादिकं प्रियविया-
गाप्रियसंयोगादिकं तन्मानसमित्युच्यते ।

No. 81.—Pain 'natural and inseparable' [No. 80] is of two
kinds, corporeal and mental. 'Corporeal' means residing in the
body; 'mental' means residing in the mind. Pain, arising from
disorder of the wind, bile, or phlegm, and taking the form of
fever, flux, cholera, swooning, &c., is called 'corporeal'. Desire,
anger, covetousness, folly, madness, envy, &c.,—privation of
what is liked and approximation of what is disliked—this is
called 'mental' [pain or evil.]

[The pain called *ádhyátmika* is that which arises from the
things called *adhyátma*—see No. 56].

अधिभूतेभ्यो भवं आधिभौतिकं । मानुषपशुम्टगसरीसृपस्थाव-
रेभ्यो दुःखमुत्पद्यते तदाधिभौतिकं ।

No. 82.—What arises from an object of sense (*adhibúta*—see
No. 56)—is called *ádhibhautika* ('natural and extrinsic'). Pain
is 'natural and extrinsic' which arises from men, cattle, wild
beasts, reptiles, or things that do not move.

अधिदेवेभ्यो जातं आधिदैविकं । श्रीतोष्णवातवर्षाश्रनिपाता-
दिनिमित्तं यद् दुःखमुत्पद्यते तदाधिदैविकं ।

No. 83.—What arises from a supernatural agent (*adhidaiva*—
see No. 56)—is called *ádhidaivika* ('non-natural' or 'superhuman'). Of this description is pain which arises from cold, heat,
wind, rain, thunderbolts, and the like.

अनेन त्रिविधेन दुःखेनाभिभूतस्य ब्राह्मणस्य जिज्ञासोत्पन्ना ।

ज्ञातुमिच्छा जिज्ञासा यथा क्षितस्य पानीयं पातुमिच्छा पिपासा ।

No. 84.—[As stated at the outset—in the mind] of the Bráhman, oppressed by the three kinds of pain, there arose 'a desire to

मस्तु ॥

No. 85.—This is saving knowledge (derived) from the compendium (of principles laid down by KAPILA.) Having known this,
there will be no further transmigration. Such is the doctrine of
the magnanimous great sage Kapila.

It is to be observed that there are in this treatise (as much as,
three hundred couplets of the *Anushthubh* metre.

Thus concludes the comment on the aphorisms called 'The
Compendium of Principles.'

86.—Of the name *Sánkhya,* which the philosophical system of
KAPILA bears, two explanations are given. According to the
one explanation, the system is so named, from the word *sankhyá*
' number,'—" because it observes precision of reckoning in the enumeration of its principles." As the word *sankhyá* also signifies " de-
liberation or judgment," the name was more probably intended to
designate the result of the " deliberate judgment" of KAPILA on
the great problem of the universe—with a special regard to emancipation from the evil that prevails in the world.

87.—The twenty-five 'principles' *(tattwa)* of the system, it
will be observed, are comprised in the first three aphorisms (No.
6.)—viz., the 'eight producers,' the 'sixteen productions,' and
' Soul.' These twenty-five principles, according to the Sánkhya,
constitute "all that is;" and KAPILA, we have seen, promises

the enquirer that his final liberation from all distress will be the result of understanding "the real nature of all that is." A noticeable distinction between Kapila's way of speaking of things, and that of the Naiyáyikas, presents itself in their respective choice of a fundamental verb. The language of the Nyáya is moulded on the verb "to be," and that of the Sánkhya on the verb "to make." The Nyáya asks "what *is*?"—the Sánkhya asks "what *makes* it so?" The one presents us with a "compte rendu" of the Universe as it stands :—the other presents as with a cosmogony. As the one subdivides its subject-matter into the two exhaustive categories of Existence and Non-existence, the other exhibits everything (except 'Soul'—the spectator of the phantasmagoria) under the two aspects of 'producer' and 'production.'

The 'productions' are held to be not other than the 'producers' modified; and the producers—all except the first of them—are but modifications of the first—the *múla-prakriti*. By what process of thought the notion of such a first principle is arrived at, the following extract from Morell's History of Philosophy (Vol. 1. p. 208), may serve to illustrate. Mr. Morell is there speaking of one of the latest German systems, that of Herbart.

88.—" The process by which the necessity of philosophy comes " to be felt is the following :—When we look round us upon the " world in which we live, our knowledge commences by a per- " ception of the various objects that present themselves on every " hand to our view. What we *immediately* perceive, however, is " not actual essence, but phenomena; and after a short time, we " discover that many of those phenomena are unreal; that they " do not portray to us the actual truth of things as they are; " and that if we followed them implicitly, we should soon be " landed in the midst of error and contradiction. For example,

" which we term things. Again, when we examine further into
" these *substances*, we discover that they are not real ultimate
" essences, but that they consist of certain elements, by the
" combination of which they are produced. What we term the
" *reality*, therefore, is not *the thing as a whole*, but the elements
" of which it is composed. Thus the further we analyse, the
" further does the idea of *reality* recede backwards; but still it
" must always be somewhere, otherwise we should be perceiving a
" nonentity. The last result of the analysis is the conception
" of an absolutely simple element, which lies at the basis of all
" phenomena in the material world, and which we view as the
" essence that assumes the different properties which come be-
" fore us in sensation."

89.—This " essence that assumes the different properties which
come before us in sensation,"—this, which the European analyst
arrives at as " the last result of the analysis"—is what the Sánkhya expositor, proceeding synthetically, lays down as his first
position. This primordial essence—among the synonymes for
which, given in our text-book (No. 7), are the ' undiscrete,' the
' indestructible,' that ' in which all generated effect is compre-
hended,' &c., is the ' Absolute' of German speculation. The
developement of this principle, according to one of Schelling's
views (noticed by Mr. Morell at p. 147 vol. 2d) is " not the free
and designed operation of intelligence, but rather a blind impulse
working, first unconsciously in nature, and only coming to self-
consciousness in mind." So, according to KAPILA, " from Nature issues Mind, and thence Self-consciousness" [see No. 54] :

—but here a striking difference between the European and the Oriental theory presents itself—for the Self-consciousness, which so many European philosophers assume as the only certain starting-point, and as the very characteristic of Soul, is declared by KAPILA to be no property of Soul, and to be regarded as such only through a delusion. In the 64th of the 'memorial verses' of I´s'WARA KRISHNA, as translated by Mr. Colebrooke, KAPILA says :—

90.—" So, through study of principles, the conclusive, incon-" trovertible, one only knowledge is attained, that neither I AM, " nor is aught mine, nor do I exist."

91.—This statement M. Cousin not unnaturally regards as amounting to "le nihilisme absolu, dernier fruit du scepticisme" —but Professor Wilson, in accordance with the commentaries, declares that "It is merely intended as a negation of the soul's " having any active participation, any individual interest or pro-" perty, in human pains, possessions, or feelings." The Soul, according to the Sánkhya, might be described in the terms in which Fichte speaks of the Mind, "as it were, an intelligent eye, " placed in the central point of our inward consciousness, sur-"veying all that takes place there"—(Morell—Vol. 2. p. 95). In the words of KAPILA (Verse 19th), "Soul is witness, solitary, " bystander, spectator, and passive." Soul being thus inert, all that is done arises from the energy of the ' radical principle'—of which one might correctly speak in the terms employed by Schelling in speaking of the ' Absolute,' where he says—" The " primary form of the Absolute is *will,* or *self-action.* It is an " absolute power of becoming in reality what it is in the germ." (Morell—Vol. 2. p. 150).

92.—The ' Absolute,' the germ, in the hands of KAPILA, hav-ing reached the form of ' Self-consciousness'—*ahankára*—the

' making of an *I*,'—the ' positing of an *Ego*'—the course of sub-
sequent developement runs parallel, for some distance, with that
followed by Fichte, who takes the 'Ego' as his starting point.
According to a writer in Brande's Dictionary—" To use the
" language of Fichte—the ego is absolute, and posits itself : it is
" a pure activity. As its activity, however, has certain indefin-
" able limits, when it experiences this limitation of its activity,
" it also posits a non-ego, and so originates the objective world.
" The ego, therefore, cannot posit itself without at the same
" time projecting a non-ego ; which, consequently, is in so far
" the mere creation of the ego." In like manner the *ahankára*
of KAPILA creates [No. 54] out of itself the five 'subtile elements,' the bases of the gross elements,—so that the world of
sense, formed out of these, is, in this as in Fichte's system, "the
mere creation of the ego." A marked difference between the
two systems, as observed before, consists in this—that KAPILA
makes the creative 'Ego' to be something else than ' Soul,' which
latter, he holds, by confounding itself with the active principle,.
gets entangled in the distresses of life.

93.—The motive of the Bráhman's enquiry at KAPILA, it will
be remembered, is this—that he wishes he may not be "again
" obnoxious to the three sorts of pain :"—in other words that he
may not be born again—that he may be no more liable to transmigration or the Metempsychosis. Of the Metempsychosis
Prof. Wilson *(Sánkhya Káriká* p. x.) says :—" This belief is not
" to be looked upon as a mere popular superstition; it is the main
" principle of all Hindú metaphysics ; it is the foundation of all
" Hindú philosophy." The doctrine of the Metempsychosis may
be regarded as the Hindú theory on the great question of the
" origin of evil." The theory may be thus stated. Evil ex-
ists—and it is not to be supposed that evil befals any one

undeservedly. When, therefore, for example, a newborn child, who has had no opportunity of acting either rightly or wrongly, is found suffering evil, it is inferred that the evil is the fruit of evil deeds done in a former state of existence. If it be asked how the person became disposed to do evil in that former state of existence, the answer offered is this—it was the consequence of evil deeds done in a state of existence still anterior—and so on. Applying now the principle of ' limits'—that what is true at every assignable point short of the limit, must be true at the limit—as there is no assignable point in the existence of evil in past time for its existence at which point this hypothesis does not serve equally well to account, it is argued that, on this hypothesis, and on no other, is the existence of evil fully accounted for. To the European this method of accounting for the origin of evil appears to be vitiated by the ' regressus in infinitum' *(ana-vasthá)*—the same consideration which vitiates the theory of the earth's resting on the elephant, the elephant's resting on the tortoise, and so on without end. The origin of evil he regards as not having been revealed; and the requirement that we shall maintain our reliance on the goodness of God in the absence of such revelation, he regards as a trial of our faith.

94.—Several of the terms in the treatise of which a translation has been given, do not occur in the Sánkhya treatises generally studied. On these and some other points a few annotations here follow.

95.—Among the epithets applied to ' Self-consciousness' (in No. 18) are *sánumána* and *niranumána.* We can get no account anywhere of this application of these terms. Self-consciousness 'not associated with inference' might possibly refer to the simple consciousness of existence ; whilst the consciousness ' associated with inference' might refer to the notion of the Egoist who has reasoned himself into the belief that he himself constitutes all that is—(see No. 17) :—but then the difficulty would remain of tracing the connexion between this sense and the functions assigned to these aspects of self-consciousness under No. 61.—The technical or 'slang' terms in Nos. 64 &c., differ in our text-book from those given in the comment on the *Kárikás*—see p. 155 of the *Sánkhya Káriká,* where Prof. Wilson says " No explanation of the words is anywhere given, nor is any reason assigned for their adoption."

96.—On the 'triad of qualities' (No. 49), Prof. Wilson, at p. 52 of the *Sánkhya Káriká,* remarks :—" In speaking of qualities, " however, the term *guṇa* is not to be regarded as an insubstantial " or accidental attribute, but as a substance discernible by soul " through the medium of the faculties. It is, in fact, nature, or " *prakriti,* in one of its three constituent parts or conditions, " unduly prominent; nature entire, or unmodified, being nothing " more than the three qualities in equipoise, according to the " Sútra, ' *Prakriti* is the equal state of goodness, foulness, and " darkness.' "

97.—The term *abhibuddhi* would seen to be obsolete in the sense assigned to it in No. 58. In the copy of the work employed in making the translation, the same term *(abhibuddhi)* is repeated as representing the first of its own five subdivisions. This, with other obvious clerical errors, has been amended with the concurrence of learned pandits. The term *karttavyatá,* in the same passage, is akin to our term ' susceptibility.'

98.—' Inference' is briefly noticed in paragraph No. 77. As the writers on the Sánkhya do not appear to be all exactly of the same mind on the subject of inference, it may be worth while to examine the matter :—and, as the terms which they make use of are the same as those which are employed, with less diversity of

sentiment, by the Naiyáyikas, it may be as well to begin by de-
termining the sense in which the Naiyáyikas understand the
terms.

99.—After describing 'perception,' in his fourth aphorism,
GAUTAMA, the founder of the Nyáya school, proceeds, in his fifth
aphorism, to speak of 'inference' as follows :—

अथ तत्पूर्वकं त्रिविधमनुमानं पूर्ववच्छेषवत्सामान्यतो दृष्ट-
च्च ॥ ५ ॥

"Now 'inference,' preceded thereby [i. e., preceded by 'perception'] is of three kinds—(1) that which has the 'prior'—(2)
that which has the ' posterior'—and (3) that which is [or consists
in] the perception of ' community.' "

100.—'Inference,' as stated in paragraph No. 77 of our text-
book, is "knowledge arising from the perception of a ' *sign ;* '"
and as the 'sign' (*linga*)—the Greek σημειον or rather τεκμηριον
—the "*mark* from which a conclusion may be drawn"—may be
of three kinds ; so the modes of 'inference,' as stated in the aphorism of Gautama, are likewise three.

101.—The first kind of 'sign' Gautama calls 'prior' (*púrvva*).
The meaning of the term is explained by his commentator (in
the *Nyáya-sútra-vritti*) as follows :—

पूर्वं कारणं । तद्दत् तल्लिङ्गकं । यथा मेघोन्नतिविश्रेषेण द-
ष्ट्यनुमानं ।

" [By the expression in the aphorism] ' prior' [is meant] *cause*
—[a cause being prior to, or the antecedent of, its effect—and,
when perceived, serving as a 'sign' of the effect yet unperceived].
[By the expression in the aphorism] 'which has that' [i. e., which
has the ' prior,' or cause—is meant] which has that as a 'sign'.

the gathering of clouds."

In this example of inference, the 'prior' (*púrvva*)—the antecedent or cause—is the 'sign ;'—the gathering of clouds, the antecedent or cause of rain, being that 'sign' from which a fall of rain is inferred by anticipation. By European writers, this kind of inference is named, in terms strictly corresponding to those of the Nyáya, inference 'a priori' [i. e. the inference of the consequent *from the antecedent*].

102.—The second kind of 'sign' Gautama calls 'posterior' (*s'esha*). The meaning of the term is explained by his commentator as follows :—

शेषः कार्य्यं। तल्लिङ्गं शेषवत् । यथा नदीवृद्ध्या वृष्ट्यनुमानं ।

"[By the expression in the aphorism] 'posterior' [is meant] *effect* [—an effect being posterior to, or the consequent of, its cause—and, when perceived, serving as a 'sign' of the cause which was unperceived]. [By the expression in the aphorism] 'which has the posterior' [is meant—inference] which has that ['posterior' or consequent] as a ' sign.' As [for example] the inference of rain from the swelling of a river".

In this example of inference, the 'posterior' (*s'esha*)—the consequent or effect—is the 'sign' ;—the swelling of a river—the consequent or effect of rain—being the 'sign' from which a fall of rain is inferred to have gone before. By European writers, this kind of inference is named, in terms strictly corresponding to those of the Nyáya, the inference 'a posteriori' [i. e., the inference of the antecedent *from the consequent*].

103.—The third kind of ' sign' Gautama calles 'the perception of community' (*sámányato drishṭa*). The import of the term is explained by his commentator as follows :—

सामान्यतो दृष्टं कार्य्यकारणभिन्नलिङ्गकं । यथा एथिवीत्वेन
द्रव्यत्वानुमानं ।

" [By inference from] ' the perception of community' [is meant
inference] where the ' sign' is other than effect or cause.   As [for
example] the inferring that something is a substance from its having the nature of earth".

In this example the *sámánya* or ' generic character' termed
prithivítwa ' earthiness' is a ' sign' from which, when perceived,
' substantiality'—neither the cause nor the effect, but, in this in-
stance, the higher genus—is inferred.   The definition applies also
to 'inference from analogy', as the term *sámányato drishṭa* has been
rendered.

104.—The commentator from whom we have quoted mentions
another opinion in regard to the names of the three kinds of
inference ;—that they refer to those three kinds of ' signs' (specified in page 38 of the ' Lectures on the Nyáya Philosophy'—)
viz., the ' sign' which is in every case present ; that which
is absent in every case but one ; and that which is present in
some cases and absent in others.   This notion—apparently origi-
nating in nothing much deeper than the consideration that there
are " three to three"—may be dismissed as barely on a level with
Captain Fluellen's parallel between Harry of Monmouth and
Alexander of Macedon, (in ' King Henry V'—Act iv—sc. 7.),
based on the consideration that " There is a river in Macedon ;
and there is also moreover a river at Monmouth".

105.—Of the three examples given in our text-book (No. 77)
the first—viz : the inferring of ' rain from the assembling of clouds,'
falls under the first division (—see No. 101.).   The second
example—the inferring that ' there is water because there are
cranes &c.', exemplifies the second division—(see No. 102)—the

class)—falls under the same head as the second—smoke being met with only where there has been fire as an antecedent. The selection of examples here therefore is unsatisfactory—being at once redundant and defective.

106.—In the 5th and 6th of the 'Memorial Verses', inference is spoken of as follows :—

———————————————त्रिविधमनुमानमाख्यातं

तल्लिङ्गलिङ्गिपूर्वकं———————————————

सामान्यतस्तु दृष्टादतीन्द्रियानां प्रतीतिरनुमानात् ।

Thus rendered by Mr. Colebrooke—

"Inference, which is of three sorts, premises an argument, and (deduces) that which is argued by it." * * * * "It is by inference (or reasoning) that acquaintance with things transcending the senses is obtained :"—

[Professor Wilson prefers rendering the latter clause thus :— "It is by reasoning from analogy that belief in things beyond the senses is attained."]

107.—The remarks of the scholiast GAUDAPÁDA (in the *Sánkhya Bháshya*) on the foregoing text are as follows :—

त्रिविधमनुमानमाख्यातं शेषवत् पूर्ववत् सामान्यतो दृष्टं चेति । पूर्वमस्यास्तीति पूर्ववद् यथा मेघोन्नत्या दृष्टिं साधयति पूर्व- दृष्टित्वात् । शेषवद्यथा समुद्रादेकं जलपलं लवणमासाद्य शेष स्यायक्ति लवणभाव इति । सामान्यतो दृष्टं । देशान्तराद्.

देशान्तरं प्राप्तं दृष्टं गतिमच्चन्द्रतारकं चैत्रवत् । यथा चैत्रनामानं
देशान्तराद्, देशान्तरं प्राप्तमवलोक्य गतिमानयमिति तद्वचन्द्र-
तारकमिति तथा पुष्पिताम्रदर्शनादन्यच्च पुष्पिताम्रा इति सा-
मान्यतो दृष्टेन साधयति । एतत्सामान्यदृष्टं ॥ किञ्च तल्लिङ्गलि-
ङ्गिपूर्व्वकमिति । तदनुमानं । लिङ्गपूर्व्वकं यत्र लिङ्गेन लिङ्गी अ-
नुमीयते यथा दण्डेन यति: । लिङ्गिपूर्व्वकञ्च यत्र लिङ्गिना
लिङ्गमनुमीयते यथा दृष्ट्वा यतिमस्येदं चिदण्डमिति ॥

"Inference, which is of three kinds, takes the name of 'that
which has the consequent' (see No. 99), 'that which has the
antecedent,' and ' that which is [or consists in] the perception of
Community.' 'That which has the antecedent,' is that [form of in-
ference] where [it is argued]—'That [which we are adducing as the
sign] is the antecedent of this [which we wish to establish] :'—
as, for example, when one proves [an approaching fall of] rain by
the rising of clouds—because this [rising of clouds] is an antecedent of rain. [As an example of inference] 'which has the consequent'—[suppose that] having found a drop of water taken from
the sea to be salt, the saltness of *the rest* also is inferred. 'Ana-
logous'—as, having observed their change of place, it is conclud-
ed that the moon and stars are locomotive like CHAITRA : that is,
having seen a person named CHAITRA transfer his position from one
place to another, and thence having known that he was locomotive,
it is inferred that the moon and stars also are locomotive. So too,
observing a mango tree in blossom, one establishes the fact that
other mango trees also are in flower [not by adducing, in proof of
the fact either, the *cause* of the fact or any *consequence* of the fact
—but] by remarking the common nature [of the mango tree under
inspection—in virtue of which common nature the other mango

' where, from a characteristic, that which possesses the characteristic is inferred,' as, [one is inferred to be] a mendicant from his staff
[when his staff is of the characteristic description carried by mendi-
cants]. And [the act of inference may be said to be] *linggipúrvva-
ka*, ' where, from what possesses a characteristic, the characteristic itself is inferred,' as, having seen a mendicant, you say, this
[which he holds in his hand, and which, from distance or some
other reason, is not clearly discernible in his grasp] is his triple
staff—[for where the mendicant presents himself, there his characteristic staff is sure to be found also]."

Now, in his example of inferring the saltness of the ocean from
the saltness of a drop taken from it, GAUDAPÁDA appears to have
been misled by the ambiguity of the word *s'esha*, which the Naiyáyikas employ as the opposite of *púrvva*—the opposition intended being that of antecedent, and consequent not that of part and
remainder. GAUDAPÁDA, taking the word in its familiar sense of
' *the rest*,' imagines that when we infer the *rest* of the ocean to be
salt like a drop taken from it, the process falls under the second
head in the division of the modes of inference, whereas it falls under
the third head—the same which he exemplifies by the case of the mango-trees. As we infer that other mango-trees blossom when one
mango-tree blossoms, because all mango-trees have one common
nature; so likewise do we infer that the other drops of the ocean
are salt, when we find that one drop is salt, because all the drops
in the ocean have one common nature. Thus, whilst our anony-
mous commentator on KAPILA gives two examples of the second
kind and no example of the third, GAUDAPÁDA gives two examples of the third kind and none of the second. For the illustra-

tion of **KAPILA**, therefore, some of his commentators would appear, by these discrepancies, to have borrowed the terminology of the Nyáya without considering themselves bound to adhere to the sense assigned to the terms by the inventors. Whether the writers on the Sánkhya, as has been suggested, intended, by their peculiar application of the terms of the Nyáya, to inculcate their own tenet of the indifference of cause and effect; is a point the consideration of which we remit to another occasion.